The Montecito Collection

Murder, Money or Mayhem in Paradise?

by

Richard Crissman

For Bernadette
who inspired the story The Big [illegible] Bar
with affection —
Dick and Alexandra
Crissman
2/8/01

Writers Club Press
San Jose · New York · Lincoln · Shanghai

The Montecito Collection

Murder, Money or Mayhem in Paradise?

Writers Club Press
an imprint of iUniverse.com, Inc.

For information address:
iUniverse.com, Inc.
5220 S 16th, Ste. 200
Lincoln, NE 68512
www.iuniverse.com

ISBN: 1-58348-778-6

Printed in the United States of America

Introduction

Not so long ago the big activity in Montecito was growing lemons and specimen trees and experimental shrubbery. Perfect climate, a touch of sea air, superb soil and shade made the best greenhouse a horticulturist could want.

And then the trains came, and winter visitors. Paradise began to slip towards merely Heavenly. The highway came slowly, for the coastal route to Los Angeles was by beach and dynamited-headlands, but the pressure was on. It is said that Easterners began the craze to own a second home in Santa Barbara, and that may be true of the Montecito end of things, but the dry fact is that most who came wanted to stay. Many visitors had the money to build, and soon houses went up the coastal shelf toward the mountains.

Because Montecito had relatively few landowners, newcomers could buy large tracts of land, suitable for building estates with tennis courts, gate lodges, and private pitch-and-puts. The scale of such building added a social dimension to this patch of Paradise.

Anything would grow in Montecito, including some towering eccentricities.

Between the wars a careful observer would be hard pressed to know whether the superb architectural efforts of the locals or their behavior were more notable. Money permits individuality like no other attribute, and there was always plenty of money in Montecito. In fact, money is the price of admission.

There is old money, held, fondled and reinvested for generations. There is a quantity of money which is 'enough', that seems to mean comfort, often elegance, and a modern disdain for what's to become of the next generation. Montecito has a few strivers, who want to be included in everything, but may lack the last million or so to quite arrive. And then there is new money. Recent fortunes take a few years of learning how to fit in, and drives up the prices of the best houses, but pretty soon blends in with the landscape.

While it takes money to get to Montecito, and money to remain, the area is remarkable for its sense of inclusiveness. Maybe it is that people enjoy new faces, maybe it is the good manners that a benign climate spawns, or maybe it is just that the Montecito people have arrived so firmly that petty snobbery melts away. Whatever, the mix of people in Montecito ranges from erudite through gorgeous and on to delightful.

People entertain each other in Montecito. Ask twelve people to dinner, and the host will see one bore who is that night able to be occasionally witty. Two beauties, two brilliant people, three young people over seventy, and four athletic people who have seen, read or experienced nearly every thing on earth.

Ask forty people for cocktails, and the host gets one amiable drunk, a Pulitzer Prize runner-up, ten beautiful women, ten retired heads of enterprises, six ladies sharing twenty divorces, two university gurus, a world-famous yachtsman and eleven grateful guests who do their best to talk to everyone else and are likely to go easy on the snacks and booze. That's congeniality.

Maybe the above suggests that the blissful backwater of Montecito could provide some material for fiction? I have thought that it does, and offer these three stories of imaginary Montecito doings accordingly. I must say, however, that my characters might occasionally resemble someone a reader may know, but that is coincidence. I am quite able to create characters entirely of my own imagining, and that is what I have done.

Contents

Dedication

These stories are affectionately dedicated to some Montecito characters who do not figure in them.

Melinda and Dean
Carolyn
Barbara
Jonathan and Eileen
Missy and Patrick
Carrie and Jim
Jim
And my own darling Alexandra.

With special thanks to the Conrads and the staff of The Santa Barbara Writer's Conference.

The cover photograph was taken by my step-son, Mark Scott-Paine. It represents the fictional Center for Historical Research, even though the actual subject is the Four Seasons Biltmore. Thanks to both of them, as well.

The Big Hershey Bar

The Big Hershey Bar

The house on the beachfront in Santa Barbara wasn't quite what it seemed. It looked like a New England salt-box from the narrow lane that ran out Fernald Point. Fernald Point? A narrow lane running backwards down the coast from a hidden turning on an improbable side road. Facing the surf, and trimmed by the Southern Pacific railroad tracks. Inverse chic at its most expensive best.

The house? A New England salt-box with a blue shingle roof and six-over-six sash windows. But not. Well set back on a narrow lot, the passer-bye saw a many-car garage with living quarters above, a cutesy arched gate leading to a graveled turnaround, and the house behind that. From the beach side, rank after rank of gables receded towards the cross-gable of the salt-box. It wasn't a house; it was a fifteen room extravaganza marching from the lane to the sea on a diagonal, so that all the rooms had a view of a slice of the broad blue Pacific Ocean. Protecting the house from the constant surge of waves, three terraces edged up the rise from the sandy beach to the gardens. Because it was California, bougainvillea, geraniums and other splashes of bright stuff smothered ordinary green things, and even at night there was color in the shadows.

There was a station wagon pulled up in the courtyard between the garage and the front door. Its windows were open to the gentle evening breeze, against which the two girl's sleeping bags gave them comfortable protection.

Behind the house, on the ocean-facing brick terrace two people were cranking up a difference of opinion into a larger issue. The man had the clothes of a wealthy sportsman, white monagrammed polo shirt, linen slacks, and tan shoes with blue saddles. He was wasting no kind words on a woman with red hair and a Victoria's Secret figure. Both man and woman held plastic glasses decorated with sea horses, mostly filled with the shrunken ice cubes of half-finished drinks. The tones of yelling and the choice of words promised that the half-finished drinks were part of a succession, not stand-alones.

Neither what was said, nor what was to happen made much difference to anyone except the girls sleeping in the back of a station wagon parked in the shrubbery at the side of the saltbox.

As the voices rose to a pitch which made the beach grasses shiver, the twelve-year old slid out of the car, leaving her younger sister curled inside the junior sleeping bag with the White Rabbit design. Lou ducked under the overgrown bushes, and toward the voices at the ocean side of the house. She had heard fights before, and understood the chaos of drunken evenings. She understood quite well enough to keep clear of whatever was going on, and to keep her sister out of the way too. But this uncle was different. He seemed to like Mom for her sober times, when she was quiet and even when she talked about the girls and their future.

'Jerry is going to take care of us, and we're going to have our own house, and we'll all be happy. He loves you two as if you were his own.' Lou and Joyce thought that Jerry was telling the truth because he was always nice to them, brought presents for them, and took an interest in whatever they said. His special treat was the big Hershey bar he brought for each girl when he came for their mother. Still, like all the uncles their mother brought home, he wanted them out of the way at their bedtime, and like all the rest, he smelled of cocktails all the time. But then, so did Mom, so that's just the way grown-ups are, she thought.

But that was why she was paying attention to tonight's quarrel. Mom and Jerry had never yelled at each other before. Lou wanted a settled life, and until now, it seemed to be on the way. But what they were saying really bothered Lou. Jerry was done with Mom, who was being called a traitor! Nothing new in being called a two-bit tramp. But traitor seemed dangerous. They shoot traitors, for God's sake!

'Couldn't wait to hop in the sack with effing Don Grunge, could you? The minute I got sick, you had his pants down, didn't you?'

Lou recognized 'got sick' for passed out, which the uncles seemed to do quite a lot. But as Mom had once explained, 'When you need a man the urge is too strong to resist. Just go for the next guy around, and nobody holds it against anyone the next day.'

Mom interrupted Jerry, screaming that at least Don could get it up, which was better than Jerry who maybe could and maybe couldn't. 'And besides his name isn't Grunge.' With that, Mom threw something at Uncle Jerry. Maybe an ashtray, because there were buts in the air and stuff hanging in the air.

Jerry grabbed the object out of the air, like a third baseman catching a fly ball. He threw it right back in Mom's direction, but aimed high, so it spun in the light from the house, and crashed out on the further terrace.

Lou's Mom said something low, which made Jerry walk over to her and pour his drink over her head. Mom, swore, but sat still to finish her drink as if nothing much had happened. Mom seemed to have calmed down, and she would pretty soon have Jerry apologizing, so maybe it would be all right again, and Lou could go back to sleep.

But no, Jerry had gone back into the house, banging the screen door behind. Lou waited, afraid Mom wouldn't get the chance to make everything all right. Lou moved closer to the window, and saw Jerry standing at a tray table, building what the uncles called a divided. A fresh drink. He drank down most of it, dividended again, picked up something from the desk drawer, and went back outside.

'Turn around Lois. I have to see your face. If you meant what you said, we're through, and I guess I am too...'

Lou shifted back into the bushes, willing her mother to say the soft things she could, but shaking for fear that she could not. She saw her mother turn, smooth some of the thrown drink off of her face, and watched rather than heard her mother repeat and embellish her insults.

Jerry reacted almost before her Mom had finished. He brought his hand to an angle with his upper arm, and Lou saw a flash and a simultaneous snap, so loud that it was over before she could think what it was. Mom's face was a blur of surprise and blood, and fell from view. Jerry raised the gun, for that was what he had had in his hand, and it flashed in the light from the house, as he seemed to move it to his own head.

Lou couldn't breathe, but made an animal sound as she reacted to her mother's faint. Faint? She'd be on her feet again, spitting back what Jerry had done to her.

Uncle Jerry heard Lou, and it made him stop what he had started. Blank-faced he saw her, swore, put down the thing in his hands, and stiffly climbed over the edge of the terrace, down to her. 'Lou. Oh Lou, poor dear. Oh Lou.' He hugged her and cried. He more than cried. He sobbed, he shook, he knelt at her feet, dropped his head so low that Lou took his face, brought it up to her level.

Lou comforted the man. 'It'll be all right. Mom says things she don't mean. She always says everything's all right in the morning. Don't cry Uncle Jerry. Don't... Here, I've been saving it. It's a Hershey Bar, well a part of one. But it's part of a big one.' Lou knew very well that her offer was ridiculous. Uncles gave Hershey bars, but none had ever eaten any. In fact, adults didn't seem to like them very much. Nor was a Hershey Bar much of a treat for her, but she had to keep up her end of the game. Men gave them, and girls were supposed to like gifts, and there it was.

Jerry took her by the hand, put her in the station wagon, and they drove off a few blocks, somewhere up in the hedgerows. The Montecito part of Santa Barbara, where you couldn't see houses, only hedges growing right up to the streets. She'd been to parties around here, watching out the car window as Mom chose a safe place to park. Then they slept until the party was over, or Mom came to take them to breakfast. Sometimes they stayed in the house where the party was. She and Joyce slept wherever they were told to, but mostly in back bed rooms. When they did that, everybody seemed to forget breakfast for them.

Lou didn't recognize the house Jerry took them to, but compared to Jerry's, it wasn't much.

Kind of a cross woman answered the door, and then some man came, spoke sharply to the woman, and the girls were sent off to bed. Very clean, but smelling a little of dampness, which is pretty much what all the beds her mother left her in smelled like. A Santa Barbara thing, her mother always said.

By morning, the man took them down towards Carpenteria, and in and through an avocado grove, and up to a school sort of place. Everyone was very polite, so Lou and Joyce were too. The Head seemed especially polite. He explained that they were to stay at 'our school' for a while, and the girls should be very happy there and would they mind having some shots and some new school uniforms. While he was speaking he moved a bowl of wrapped miniature candies towards the girls. Little Baby Ruth bars, Mars Bars and Hersheys to choose from. They both took the Hersheys.

The Head talked some more, making it clear to the girls that he was planning for their long future.

Joyce tuned up to whimper about Momma and when was she coming, but Lou put the kibosh on that. 'Mom will come for us whenever she gets the chance. So pipe down, will you? It's baby stuff, and after all, she always comes, doesn't she?'

Thereafter, neither girl spoke of their mother. Joyce seemed content with the regularity of life at school, and the kindness of the dorm mother went a long way with her. Lou moved along on the surface of their life. She wasn't any more than content. Regular meals, daily schoolwork, church on a regular basis, and nighttime prayers were fine. But she realized that her mother wasn't coming back, that Jerry had done something so that Mom would not come back. What Jerry had done, she could not consider, and she deliberately rubbed out what she remembered of it.

Nor did anyone mention Uncle Jerry.

The Westbourne School status remained quo for four neutral years. Lou tended towards dutiful and rather rote performance in classes, which earned 'A's regularly. Joyce had more fun, and managed respectable 'B's and a largish popularity. The girls were invited to the homes of other students for holidays, and made friends of both the superficial and lasting sorts. Parents tended to remember Lou as, 'So thoughtful and pleasant,' and Joyce as 'Such fun to have over the holiday!'

During the long summer vacations, the girls went to dude ranches where there were good horses and pure lakes, and they went with the unwanted children of rather rich parents. They knew they had nothing much as allowances, but they accepted as usual the luxuries of these camps and lodges. If any of the girls' friends wondered about their background or the ability of their guardians to pay for all of this, everyone was too well mannered to ask. Even so, Lou knew it was a little unreal. If Mom had made it up with Jerry, why hadn't they been sent for? Jerry, so interested, was apparently out of the picture. Lou said to herself that she was treading water. Waiting for word from Mom. And then she told herself that Mom was dead. That Jerry had shot Mom, and that she wouldn't think about that ever again. But she did. She ran the loop of that film of the terrace at Fernald Point through her mental projector pretty often, and willed forgetfulness about as often.

During short holidays, the Head and his wife did their best for the six or eight girls who boarded, and had no nearby homes to go to. They made picnics to take to the beach or treks to take the girls up into the mountains. In either case, the Westbourne picnic was chicken salad sandwiches, celery and carrot sticks, an apple, and Hershey bars, the no-nuts kind on account of braces. Hershey bars were nice, but didn't make up for going home. If they had one.

During an Easter vacation of that first year, the girls had stayed with the W. Humphrey Smith family. The Smiths were a big disorganized, cheerful lot. There were several servants who seemed to take a lot of TV breaks, two boys who owned every piece of sports equipment ever made, and four girls who seemed to own only new clothes. There were horses out at the polo field, and a sailboat in the harbor. Breakfasts were a buffet of cold cereals and canned fruit left on the pantry sink by one of the maids. Lunch never seemed to happen at all, and dinner was a cheerful riot. Microwave packages, put in and removed by several youngsters, lots of ice cream, and a rare salad were what Lou remembered. But most of all she remembered the laughter. Six children, mostly absent servants and meals with laughter as the chief course.

The gin smell of the host and hostess seemed normal to Lou, and their elaborate courtesy to each other seemed safe: they never seemed to disagree. Lou wondered what they would ever have to differ about? Neither Smith noticed the children except as equals at the dinner table, but they seemed to enjoy them enormously, even so. Pretty much as children among children. Lou liked the Smiths, and it was a place she hoped they would be invited to again.

Her special memory of the Smith place was a stone mounting block, which was rather lost in a planting of seasonal flowers down at the far end of the lawn. She didn't know it was a step to help a rider climb onto a horse. Nor did she know that Mr Smith had brought it to California when he and Mrs Smith had moved out many years before. It said 'Smith Farm' because that was the name of the children's grandfather's enormous summer estate in Massachusetts. Mr Smith had loved the Farm, but had to agree to sell it when he and his sister split their parents' assets. But for that he would never have come to California.

For Lou, sitting on the cool stone, surrounded by the odors of the flowers, looking up that long lawn towards the happy house, it was a secure place. A place she would always remember.

When the Head, about four years after the girls had come to Westbourne, explained that the school had, reluctantly, to ask them to stop being boarding students, it was a change they didn't question. Lou hoped for nothing, but Joyce said that Jerry and Mom had sent for them.

No one had sent for them, Lou found out. The school asked Mrs Smith for help, and she, well aware that money was scarce in her household, simply asked the girls to move in, because that would be, she reasoned, less expensive than paying their board. Mr Smith seemed a little surprised at having two more children so abruptly, but Peggy said it was only fair, especially as they had an extra bedroom. Mrs Smith quieted Mr Smith's misgivings by saying that it was an economy, because all they would be paying was the day tuition, the same as he paid for their other children. Smith looked at his wife as if he thought she might be putting something over on him, then smiled, because he could see that she wasn't.

It seemed odd to Lou to move to the Smiths, but she accepted the change because she had no idea what else to do. Joyce was, however, enthusiastic. She liked the Smith girls, and admired the two older Smith boys, who seemed quite sophisticated.

The Smiths lived in a big and untidy Shingle Style house about three blocks above Coast Village Road, in Montecito. The house was brown, the eves deep and former owners seemed to have enclosed porches and alcoves of the house in a random way. What had begun life as a carefully designed summer home for some Chicago people around 1912 had become a looming pile of shadows, with big porch windows here and there like misplaced eyes. Bountiful flowers, almost ten acres, some amazing old trees, and the cheerful noise of all the occupants made the place a warm shelter from real life beyond the gates. Gate. Only one wing of the gates worked, the other being damaged and propped open because of a late-evening encounter with Mr Smith, one evening some years before.

The Smiths main demand upon their children was that they dress like Brooks catalogs. Of almost equal importance was church on Sunday, followed by lunch at the Club. On Sunday, manners were obligatory, even if at all other meals the shying of a roll or flick of water from a teaspoon seemed part of the evening banter.

The Smith's administration of the house was chaotic. Or non-existent. A man named Vogel paid the bills when he could get the money together to do it, and only then if Mr Smith was in the mood to be bothered. The tuitions of six children were paid irregularly and usually in arrears. Six polo horses, a day-sailor, servant's wages, also paid in arrears, insurance, and huge liquor and grocery bills, not to mention clothing charges rather limited the applications of income from a generous amount of capital. And of course, there were taxes, which did get paid, thanks to a ruthless attitude on Vogel's part.

The main maid, Nadia, did as she liked about everything, running the second maid ragged with picking up six, now seven bed rooms, each with it's own bath. No Smith ever picked up anything. Whatever was dropped had to be cleared away before Mrs Smith saw it; it was her only interest in housework: it had to look orderly

Joyce and Lou enjoyed being nearly-Smiths. Belonging to a family as easy as the Smiths was soothing and safe.

Exploring the big old house was a novelty. One huge enclosed porch housed only a Ping-Pong table. Another after-thought enclosure had stacks of National Geographics and Book-of-the-Month items going back about twenty years. Mostly still in their shipping wrappers. But neatly piled, of course.

There was a big dining room with a plastic cloth on the table and some flowers in cheap glass vases, stacks of paper napkins, and crocks with real silver knives, forks, several kinds of spoons, and a metal tray of serving spoons. The Gorham Silver Company would not have recognized their most expensive pattern of sterling silver; it was cloudy white from years of the Heavy Soil cycle of the dishwasher. Behind the dining room, there was a pantry with glass cabinets full of elaborate crystal and fluted plates, a kitchen, several rooms beyond that whose use Lou could not guess, and then three rooms which Nadia called the laundry room.

There were baskets of dirty clothes stacked, but neatly, in each room. A vast ironing table was covered with clothes in baskets. The washing machine room was banked with them, and the drying room…no machine dryer, only elaborate adjustable clotheslines raking from side to side in a well-ventilated space was also banked with storage baskets of clothes. Old sweat, stale perfume and other odors lingered to the point that Lou guessed that laundry was not actually done here.

She asked Nadia how it was best to wash clothes and was told to leave her stuff on the floor. When Lou ran out of clothes, she asked Peggy Smith when would the laundry come back.

Peggy looked surprised. "I don't know.' She had never thought of soiled clothes as coming-back. 'If you need something Mother is going to Nordstrom's. Come on and we'll get something we like.'

That's the way it was at the Smiths. Always new clothes if you left anything on the floor. And if Joyce and Lou put stuff back in the closet, or the bureau, it was still dirty the next time they wanted it. Lou went down to use the washer, but she had to ask Junior how, because she had never used one herself.

Junior had never run one either, and took the invitation to go with this pretty girl into a dark and disused room as an invitation. He doused the overhead lights, told Lou she was the hottest thing he had ever seen, at the same time trying to insert his hand into her T-shirt at the back. His other hand roamed (inaccurately) up her front. The sweat and stale cosmetic odors were too much like her memories of her mother's energetic reception of Uncle this, or Uncle that, and the sounds of passion that came from her bedroom, which had smelled sort of like the Smith's pile of unwashed clothes. She said that she wasn't standing for this, and she expected to be treated like a sister even if she was only a guest.

Junior backed off, muttering that it was just for fun, and how else was a man to know if he didn't try. After that, Junior treated her with elaborate respect. At first it was teasing, but it grew into reverence for his nearly-sister's smarts. They were friends, and Junior trusted Lou as he trusted no one else.

Joyce had been too flat chested, too young to attract any attention from the boys, and had been lost among the four young Smith girls. That was fine, as she badly needed the sense of belonging to some group, and the Smiths were inclusive.

The family was amply fed, and every one of the children contributed to the boisterous dinner times. The riot began in the kitchen, during which the senior Smiths perched with Martini pitcher on bar stools, encouraging this or that Smith to rally round and get the dinner into and out of the microwave. Then the plates and food moved to the dining room. The Seniors brought their drinks to the table in a fresh pitcher, refereed the chatter of news, mutual insults and jokes. And drank. They regarded the food their children ate as their appetizers. A snack here, a spoonful there. When the young people had finished with ice cream, and the dishes had been parked in the sink for the maid to do the next day, the seniors made a fresh pitcher. Then they followed the children upstairs, kissed them all soundly goodnight, and retreated to their own bedroom to watch TV, finish the Martinis and pass out.

But that was not necessarily the end of the night. Junior had long since discovered that his parents' supervision of the dinner hour was too blurred to distinguish whether he was having a glass of ginger ale at the table, or a beer. He preferred beer. And one beer led to another, and finally to a half-keg in his closet. When Lou found out what was going on, she told Junior to oust the beer. He retaliated late at night in turning her door knob, or making panting sounds on the porch that ran between his parents room and the room Lou and Joyce shared. This seemed pretty harmless to Lou, as the door was locked and the Smith's were, after all, there to protect her. It escaped her that Junior had walked through his sleeping parents' room to get on to the shared porch. Finally, Lou carried Junior's beer into his bathroom, turned on the tap, and drained the half-keg. He laughed when he saw what she had done, but something about her mouth told him that the next keg would go the same way, so he never got another.

Lyman Smith, however, came to be a different matter. He had learned to buy videos from a catalog. His oblivious father never opened mail until the day after it came, so Lyman simply ordered films in his father's name, with his father's credit card, and when they came along, usually after lunch when Senior was either still in the bar at the club, or resting from that excursion,

Lyman removed the package from the mail. He had thus built a large and explicit library of films for his private viewing. Lyman had a tower sort of bedroom, and although he shared a bath with his older brother, he was far too careful to let his brother in the room. Junior had swiped Lyman's science project several years before, and Lyman learned to exclude Junior. All Junior knew about Lyman was that he watched an awful lot of TV in his room after dinner.

Lou was invited to Lyman's room to watch some TV one evening after the Seniors had retired, and Junior was at the movies with some friends. Unsuspicious, Lou had sat in an old wicker chair in Lyman's room, watching a mildly erotic flick with him when he said something like, 'Kid stuff,' and changed cassettes. It took a minute or two for Lou to see where the picture was going, but as soon as she got the idea, she said that she didn't want to watch, only to find that Lyman had locked the door.

'Either let me out, or I'll scream, and your sisters can explain it all to your parents.'

Lyman laughed. 'They've all seen my pictures, so they don't care about you being a professional virgin. They don't give a rat's ass one way or another about you. So just shut up and enjoy the pretty pictures. Lyman was rubbing his stomach under his polo shirt, with the intention of rubbing himself a little lower down in a minute or two. Just to get her warmed up, he told himself.

Lou was at the window, figuring how much of a jump the bushes below might be when Mollie drummed on the door. 'Lyman, let me in. Right now you creep. I know that Lou is in there, and she's probably as pissed at you as I am.'

Lou answered that Mollie had it right.

Lyman produced the key, slammed and re-locked the door after them, and returned to his favorite activity. The girls giggled, told each other that Lyman was harmless, but sick in the head, and forgot about the incident.

The daily maid, whose pay was sometimes erratic, was glad not to have to deal with Lyman's room. In fact, Nadia Cruz, the head maid, thought it indecent that each Smith child had their own room, and now the two new children had their own room to boot, and every last one of them a TV and VCR besides. But Mrs Smith didn't notice that the house was never clean, only picked up, so she was easy to work for. It had to look neat, but that was the Smiths only requirement. Dropped clothes and sports equipment went on to the pile in the laundry room. When the youngsters complained that they were out of this or that garment, whichever parent had the time took the complaining child to either Nordstrom's or W.A. King to buy replacements. Of course some clothes might have been handed down as the children grew, but on the whole, the smaller clothes were on the bottom of the heap in the laundry room, and so, non-existent.

This benign policy was extended to Lou and Joyce, and after they realized that neither would ever see clean clothes again, both enjoyed the freedom of enlarging their wardrobes at will. Lou felt they were leaning rather too much on the Smith's generosity, but her small effort to wash her own clothes was nipped in the bud when Nadia spotted her sorting clothes in the laundry room. The unwashed clothes were reserved for Nadia's nephews and nieces, making draperies for her aunt's apartment, and providing attractive bed sets for her own room. The laundry room was for raiding, not for washing, Nadia explained, so get the heck out of here.

After Nadia had effectively forbidden Lou to try to organize the laundry, she began to take a greater interest in cooking, often preparing a dish of something from scratch materials. No one much noticed, though, because the household lived on large packages of discount prepared foods and instant stuff. But Lou liked doing it better than lying around all day watching TV, or endlessly hanging out at the beach. Gradually she expanded her repertory to the point that she had to ask for ingredients that Nadia never bought.

"Christ Lou, can't you leave me alone. I got enough to do buying what they can cook without I have to buy special for you. Mrs. Smith don't want to be bothered, and I don't neither. So cool it."

Lacking money and transportation, Lou's range of movement was pretty narrow. Montecito's Upper Village was less than a quarter of a mile from the Smiths. Walking carefully along the verges of the narrow lanes which hold Montecito together like the veins of leaves, Lou went directly to the three restaurants in the cluster of tile-roofed shops which make up the Village. At the first two, her offer to work from four to seven every night was declined with amusement.

'Rich girl showing off,' both managers thought.

La Golandrina was expensive, casual and always short staffed because the owner's temperament required mute slaves. He rattled the timid, and fired the combative. Four to seven was a short shift, but the girl could do a lot of skut work before the serious business of the kitchen came up. For Lou, the little job was freedom. Fifteen hours gave her sixty-five a week for herself. She was home, at the Smiths, in time to participate in the free-for-all of the dinner hour, and in plenty of time to get her homework done. She was offered any of the activities the Smith children had, but no one noticed that she ducked out of everything but weekend horse activities. Lou made an allowance of twenty a week to Joyce, and saved most of the rest of her money.

Walking home at seven o'clock was fine in the summer, but a winter evening among the overhanging cypress and sweet-olive hedges of Montecito was not so pleasant. For one thing, the lanes were as dark as lightlessness could make them. Cars hummed past, not seeing her slim body pressed against the hedges. One night a shiny car of some kind crowded Lou into a hedge, the window slid down, and a man who seemed terribly old to Lou asked if he might have the pleasure of driving her home.

'Thanks' she said, 'I live right here,' and she suited her actions to her lie, and turned in at the next drive. She stood in the dark for a few minutes, heard the car turn, drive back, and finally accelerate. The man had been someone she had seen in the village. A man who watched girls too closely. Creepy. Men were that way, she decided, fortified by her mother's view of the need for and uselessness of men for any other purpose than sex. She considered whether she could do without them.

Joyce was thirteen when she complained about the allowances the four Smith girls got. A fifty-dollar bill every Saturday that Mr Smith remembered to get them, which was most of the time. Rather routinely the money was left on the dinner table. Lou and Joyce had always been afraid to take one, and the Smiths were too absent-minded to notice that they hadn't provided anything for them. Lou forbade Joyce to complain, but Peggy Smith intervened. 'It's not like they don't want to do it, but we have to remind them about everything.' Still, weeks went bye, and nothing was left for the Fuller girls.

Then Mollie, the oldest Smith girl got a car. It was only a used one, but convertible, and stylish. She asked for and got a hundred for her expenses, provided she took on some driving of the younger girls back and forth from school.

'But Dad, you never give Lou and Joyce an allowance. It's not fair to raise Mollie and still keep Lou and Joyce out of it!' Peggy said. She was next oldest to Mollie, and a keen champion of any under-dog.

'No, dear, I get the same amount every week, fifty for every girl, except now Mollie gets more. You just have forgotten.'

'Dad! How many girls live here?'

'Don't get Bolshy old girl. There are six of you. Oh, mmm, of course Lou and Joyce! Did I leave them out? What? I never meant to, never on earth. I guess I must owe you girls some big sum. Let's see, two years at fifty a week…umm…that's pretty stiff. Tell you what, I'll give you each a thousand to make it up, and you may both have a hundred a week until I make up the rest. Is that fair?'

Only Lou figured it out correctly. They had lived there three and a half years, not two. Even so, she kept silent, willing Joyce not to correct Mr Smith. It wouldn't be wise to remind the Smiths of their generosity, any more than it would be smart to comment upon the careless affection which left all the Smith children about as overlooked as the Fuller girls.

About the time Joyce had blown her thousand in full, mostly in loans to Smith children or gifts to anyone who seemed to need it, the Smiths got in a jam. Mr Smith was pulled over on the way home from a dance at the Club.

Montecito is not a town, only a disconnected part of Santa Barbara County. As County, its police force is the Sheriff's Department. Even though the officers are rotated within the County area, the Deputies get to know prominent citizens, scofflaws and ordinary malfeasants. Even so, Sheriff's Deputy Leo Garcia was truly frightened by what he had to do.

He had known the Smiths for years, each by name, all by address, and Junior and Lyman by repeated warnings about juvenile hi-jinks. The senior Smiths were about as nice as anyone he had ever met, even if they were sort of town drunks. He sure didn't want any blame over them, but they were out meandering all over East Valley Road, and he couldn't let the old gent drive any more. It was his fifth warning, and if he didn't get them, Breaker Morgan, the meanest Deputy, would get them sometime, and really stiff it to them. So Leo had to act, just for their own good. When he had their attention, and they stopped, he had to ask Mr Smith to, 'Please, sir, breathe in here.' The breathalyzer gave a high reading, and Leo told his partner, 'Christ. Damned if I do, and shit if I don't.'

Smith breathed in and out of the blue balloon with courtesy and patience, which did not save him. He was cited for driving under the influence, and the officer kindly suggested that the Smiths leave their car in a side turning, and allow the officers to drive them home. This seemed likely to work until Mrs Smith opened her car door, and fell face first out her door. She skinned her wrists and palms, and hit her head a very loud crack- Leo summoned an ambulance.

Smith said, 'Thank you for your courtesy, officer, we can walk from here.' Gravely bidding the officer good night, they set off down the road. Scared sick, Leo Garcia walked with them, flashing his flashlight to warn traffic. After about ten yards, the patrol car began to follow with all lights flashing. At the head of the procession, Mrs Smith's lacquered curls caught the light. Her diamond bracelet flashed another kind of signal, and her tasteful gray chiffon dress moved well with her steady gait. Smith's progress was equally dignified, until both Smiths, having exchanged a word or two, turned into a planting of dark green pittosporum and simply and without warning, sat down in the dirt. Even sitting, leaning into each other's shoulders, they were dignified. Even totally unconscious they had aplomb.

The next morning, Judge Walter Custine received the Smith's lawyer and Deputy Garcia in his chambers. A very starched shirt-sort of townie representing the Smiths opened the meeting with expressions of gratitude to the police for not booking them. Then he took a long time to explain just who the W. Humphrey Smiths were in terms of social, financial and intellectual achievement.

Custine held up his hand after the thirtieth paragraph. 'This is, excuse me Mrs Smith for being so blunt. This is bullshit and we all know it. I'll make you a deal. Both of you surrender your licenses right here and now. Officer Garcia is quite forgetful, and I am very forgiving. But I don't forget. So here's the deal. Neither of you ever drives again. Right? And you, Mr Smith can afford a driver, and I expect you to get one. Right? And both of you are famous in Santa Barbara for being drunks, so I'm sentencing you to one hundred hours of community service, which may, and hopefully will be worked off helping AA run meetings.

At home that evening, Martini glass in hand, Mr Smith made the best of it. 'We have reached the age when it is no longer safe for your mother or me to drive a car. Accordingly, Junior, you may have the Mercedes. You will drive me as needed.'

Junior loudly complained about his busy schedule with the junior race weekend at the Yacht Club, and that working the horses took all the rest of his time, and besides he had no intention of giving up his Jeep.

Smith relented quickly. 'At your age I had a Chrysler convertible, and very snappy it was. I guess I can't blame you for not wanting a black Mercedes sedan.'

No one considered asking Lyman who had a Mustang and kept it in perpetual motion between UC Santa Barbara and UCLA, where his current girl friend went to school. Peggy Smith was to have Mrs Smith's Cadillac Allante, which she claimed by right of needing a convertible.

Lou said that she was out of school early most days, and could be counted upon for any driving which they needed.

Mr Smith pushed the Mercedes keys at her, saying, 'Well, that's done. Thank you Lou, that's going to be very helpful. Now, Mother, shall I fix a little dividend?'

'Yes, thank you dear. But we still need a driver for parties and Los Angeles trips.'

'Ask Twitvogel,' Senior said expansively, 'He'll know a service.'

Twit was Victor. Victor Vogel was the long-suffering accountant who paid the Smiths bills and kept them afloat. Tall, lean and quiet. Vogel tended to listen with his mouth open, either suggesting he had his adenoids, or that he wanted to drink in every nuance of the other person's wisdom. He was a young-looking fifty-something, actually fairly athletic, but dressed to look half-asleep. Long before Armani wrapped the male form in tubular black stuff, Vogel had been buying extra-long suits, which buried his six-feet in stiff suiting. He seemed positively avuncular to Lou, who in fact, was quite careful of younger men.

Vogel picked over the bills Lou had been sent with, saying, 'Most expensive ten people in Montecito. Their food and liquor bills would feed any other gang's army.' The next time Lou brought bills, he apologized. 'There's no one else in that zoo who has a lick of sense. I guess I got carried away when I heard a reasonable question. Sorry. Now about these bills. Did you really have ten pork loin roasts last month? Uh, uh and six primes of beef?'

'What bill is that, Mr Vogel?'

'Upper Village Market. Isn't that where you shop?'

"No, I don't do the shopping, Nadia does. And there's no one knows how to cook those things. We eat Smart and Final and Costco things, like lasagna and heroes, or spaghetti. Sometimes we have fish sticks. But I've never seen anything like meat for a meal at home.'

'Nadia Cruz signed for the meat. Here's the slips.' Vogel spread about fifteen charge slips on the table, and slid them over to Lou. 'Just take a look at the Nordstrom bill. Did one of the boys get a tailcoat last month? And a ball gown for nine hundred ninety five dollars? Most Smiths get men's clothes at W.A. King, and you girls get fancy clothes in Beverly Hills. Is someone at last trying to cut down?'

Lou thought for a minute. 'I don't want to mix everything up. The Smiths get along fine with Nadia, and I don't think that they ought to be upset with this.'

'But you agree that Nadia is stealing from the Smiths?'

'Nadia's niece was married last month. I don't think this will ever come up again. But you could close the market account. We never have that kind of food, anyway. I could take over the shopping, if they agree. And I think I can talk to Nadia so it will work out without going to Mrs Smith. She likes Nadia, you know.'

Vogel said that was a lot for her to do, but it might help. 'There have to be some economies. They spend way more than comes in, and we have to sell stock to cover the bills. Thank god the remaining stocks go up in value about covering what we have sold. But it's a bad scene. And there's no way I can squeak out another dime for anything, so no more cars for anyone. Just be glad they're letting you have the Mercedes, you'd never a car otherwise. Jeez. Why can't those kids get jobs and pay their own allowances!'

That week Lou had her talk with Nadia. Amid tears and apologies, Nadia admitted feeding the wedding party and outfitting the bridal party. Not just the ball gown for the bride, but six other dresses, and matching cases of liquor from Costco which no one ever noticed. In return for immunity, Nadia turned over the shopping to Lou, and surrendered her charge cards. She agreed that the nieces and nephews would whip through all that laundry, and sort it out. Almost five years of sheets and clothes reappeared, much of it outgrown, and some of it being replacements for replacements.

The younger Smiths marveled at half-chickens for a change, and homemade casseroles, and salads tossed at home instead of bought at four bucks a pound in the deli department. Within six months, every bill in the house had plunged lower than next year's neckline. About the only bills that were unchanged were liquor, Club bills and stable bills. Even the gasoline bills went down because Nadia and her husband had to buy their own now.

Encouraged by this trend, Vogel called the Smiths and asked if he could come over within a day or so. He said he had a proposition to put to them.

'Of course, Smith said, 'Come for cocktails. Say fiveish.'

'How about four?'

'Good God man, we never have cocktails before five.'

Vogel tried to explain that he wanted a business meeting, not drinks.

Rather shocked, Smith said that, very well, he could come at eight for dinner, and skip the drinks.

Not knowing what he had let himself in for, Vogel accepted.

Mr Smith forgot to tell anyone a guest was coming because whoever came to dinner was fine with him, but Lou found out about it from Vogel. She asked Mrs Smith if she could make a pretty table for their guest.

'Of course my dear. We always used to have a well-set table. That was when we had Holman, but of course he left to work for the Kirklands. That was before their divorce, and then he went to the Palmer Hoyts, who moved you know. I guess we just got out of the habit. But you mustn't make too much of Mr Vogel. He just does books and things you know. But very nice and all.'

Lou set out crystal that was fogged by years of disuse, and colorfully painted plates, and some crystal candlesticks because the silver ones took too long to clean. When she finished, the table looked the way Uncle Jerry's table looked when Mom ever got around to setting it. Not that Lou intended the result, but that was the only table she had ever seen set, except at school.

The Smiths were full of praise, especially the girls who said that this was more like it. Mrs Smith swooped around the table correcting the lay of some of the forks and glasses, and said it looked very well.

Mr Smith said that the plates looked good enough to eat off of, which he thought was pretty funny.

When Vogel arrived, the Smiths were delighted to offer one last round of drinks, after which serious conversation was clearly impossible. Still, the lively chatter of, that evening, six girls and two young men at the table, and the Smiths, who encouraged world events and social issues at the table surprised Vogel. Few families had such interests, and fewer had parents who so carefully brought out the ideas of each girl. Nearly drunk they may have been, but they were very good parents, he concluded.

Lou had served tomato bisque to begin, her poached chicken with shallots and mushrooms, green beans made the way Julia Childs recommended, and a salad of mixed greens with slabs of Camembert cheese as a last course. Even the Smiths ate some of every dish, so that by the end of the meal they were in pretty good shape.

Vogel cleared his throat, and Smith asked if he had some speech to make, expecting to get a laugh.

'Actually, sir, I do. And I hope I may say what I have to say in front of your children.'

Smith twisted his napkin onto the table. 'You may speak before my children, there's no need for them to turn so that they may be in front of you. Just go right ahead.'

The girls knew that one, but produced the expected giggle.

Vogel said that he wanted to discuss the family finances. He reviewed the gross family income, a figure that shocked Lou deeply. It was so much! Then, he explained the amount of taxes, and indicated the deficit. When he explained that instead of the inheritances growing as he was sure the Senior Smiths hoped, the estate was barely keeping its gross value.

'Well I know all that, and I've told the girls and their brothers all about it dozens of times. So we have to thank you for your diligence, but actually I can't see what good it does to keep tramping through the numbers.' Smith swirled his Martini gently, looked at it, and polished it off.

'Daddy, you did warn us when Holman left, but that was six years ago. We all thought that saving money on Holman made everything all right again.' Mollie looked at Vogel for agreement.

Lyman added, '...unless you have some other solution.'

'Thanks. I do have a suggestion, and it's because doing without Holman didn't save anything at all.'

There was an uproar about that, because Holman's era had come to be regarded as a time of good meals and clean clothes and manicured hedges. They gave him up to right the financial ship, and now Vogel claimed it was sinking again.

When Vogel got the floor again, he said that what the house needed was a firm hand in the executive department. 'Bills have gone way down since Lou took over the buying and cooking. And the bills for new clothes, sheets and towels had practically vanished since Lou and, ah-mmm Nadia had reorganized the laundry room.'

'And damn fine job she's made of it. Right girls?'

They agreed with their father.

Vogel rushed to the end of his report, saying that it was time to put Lou in formal charge of all the household bills. 'She should be delegated to talk turkey to Junior and Lyman about harbor and horse bills because I don't understand anything about any of that.'

'Well, for goodness sakes Vogel, I'm perfectly capable of talking to my own boys. And besides, young men are always extravagant. I certainly was myself, but look at me now. I hardly ever spend a penny on myself. We men grow out of it!'

'Daddy, you'd give either Junior or Lyman the moon if they asked for it, and each of us too. But it's just too cruel if we spend our capital and have to actually work all our lives. You must see that!'

'Work?' Mrs Smith was surprised. 'Surely we'll never come to that! There's so much else to do…' Mrs Smith seemed to realize that she had said something silly, and continued, 'Of course you girls must have careers and go to university like the boys . But you must have enough capital so that you have choices about things, isn't that right Mr Vogel? Anyway, I think you are right. Lou has the most common sense of any of us, and she's a perfect dear. Do you know that when Nadia went and charged her wedding to us, Lou made her pay it all back? Well, not in cash, but in laundry and such. Nadia told me, and I felt so glad that Nadia confessed that I gave her that ugly emerald frog that we got in Hong Kong.

Such a waste of money, I simply can't wear green. And Lou settled the whole thing with no hurt feelings whatsoever.'

'It was Nadia's niece's wedding, and I told her we would contribute the champagne if she would choose a California brand. I hope nothing happened that looked like I reneged on my gift.' Mr Smith looked good-humoredly at Lou, who shook her head. 'So that's all right then. If Vogel is satisfied, then so are the rest of us. Girls? Joyce? You get a say too. You are one of us, you know.'

Vogel tried to escape, but the Smiths decided upon Gin Alexanders, and Vogel simply had to stay for at least one, they declared.

Vogel made one last try. 'I would urge all of you young people to get a job, and make a little of your own spending money, the way Lou does.'

Shock. No one in the family knew that Lou had a job. The Smiths dined at their club, at other people's houses or at home, and the children ate at the club snack bar or at home. No one had the cash to go to a restaurant, but Vogel, who knew how to manage his own money, did eat out. He had spotted Lou.

Mr Smith again apologized for his oversight about allowances, while everyone else said they had never noticed her being gone.

Lou said, 'It wasn't just for money. You see, I just feel better when I'm busy. I guess I just don't have the knack for playing, like the rest of you have. Sorry if I did anything wrong.'

Junior began a spirited defense of himself as not playing when he was destructing and rebuilding his sailboat or training his horses. 'I made money on both horse trades this year.'

Vogel said that might make the polo deductible, if it sometimes yielded a profit, and asked if Junior regarded horses as a business. This detour took the spotlight off of Lou, and oddly, no one ever spoke of Lou's job again. It was so unfamiliar a topic as to have dropped out of sight in all eight of the Smith's memories. Work? None of them ever had, nor ever would. But Lou, alone in a crowd, always worked for money, saved her money, and, in the end, was the richest for having worked.

The evening had not ended, however. To the complaint that the Smith's couldn't really afford to continue as they were, Smith said, 'We already have the life we can afford. So kindly don't lecture me on small economies. That's what brought on the depression. People stopped spending.'

'It's not what you spend, it's what you waste,' Vogel persisted.

'How can I get a car? The rest of this is just bull,' Lyman offered.'

'Language!' remonstrated Senior. Mrs Smith poured herself a dividend and otherwise ignored the gathering.

Lou spoke up. 'I volunteered to help, and if everyone will go along with it, we'll be just fine, won't we Mr Vogel?'

'Pretty much, if you all kept it up.'

'What? Do what?' Mrs Smith asked.

Lou, joined by Junior, explained. The senior Smiths waved it all off as if the matter were of Einsteinian consequence, and thus impenetrable. Junior, however, made more bold by the beer he had in his glass of ginger ale, encouraged the rest of the children to back him, and Joyce fell in, more or less because she wanted some independence from her sister's drumming practicality.

'For the Lord's sakes, do whatever you want,' Senior conceded, 'just let's get on with it.' Which seemed to mean that the Smiths had a little dividend of brandy Alexander and excused themselves from the first dinner party they had given in some years.

Vogel winked at Lou as the rest of the young people made stacks of dishes and cleared stuff to the sink. 'And what will you do with your power, Lou?'

'Can I do practically nothing except save money? It's not up to me to run the Smiths, but I think I'm supposed to see that they get their money's worth. Any way, that's all I'm going to try to do.'

'But you can't do your job at La Golandrina and run the house too, can you?'

Vogel looked so concerned that Lou almost laughed. 'Try me. Just give me the chance.'

And so, for a punishing six months, the household had clean clothes, the Nordstrom's bill shrank, and food cost about eight dollars a day per person. Grudgingly, Nadia kept up her end of things, until, one night, Mrs Smith said, 'Well, this is the way we used to live. Imagine! Nadia was so worn out she really couldn't cope. She needed your help. We really appreciate you, Lou. Truly.' She lifted her glass, one of the better ones that Lou now routinely provided for the cocktail tray.

Junior appreciated having some respect for being in the horse business. He invited Lou for a ride to demonstrate his new trail horse, and he intended to show her what a superior sort of jock he was. Lou, once again, had to demonstrate that she was not falling for his machismo, and Junior was a reformed character where she was concerned. All that actually happened was that she kneed him painfully in a tender private spot, and said he should use better judgement: her jaw was clamped in that special way that he understood. The final blow was that Lou said of Jingo, the horse in question, that he didn't respect Junior. In fact, after hearing that analysis from Lou, Jingo tossed Junior right over his head.

Lou was very busy driving Mrs Smith to get her nails and hair done, and to bridge at the club. Junior was pretty good with his father, but towards Fall, his class schedule picked up, and Lou had Mr Smith to ferry as well as Mrs Smith. Getting them to the club by lunch time, getting them home, getting to work, and back to orchestrate dinner was a full afternoon for Lou, but she never missed school in the morning. She cut, but mostly passed her afternoon classes, partly because the faculty at Westbourne knew the load she was carrying. But, senior or not, Lou did her homework and avoided the distractions of Senior Prom, Graduation, college recruiting and glandular impatience.

The Mercedes sedan gave her a freedom she cherished. A big Hershey bar of her own, she told herself. The reward for being a good girl.

Her luxury vehicle did not go unnoticed, even among the affluent at Westbourne School. Offers of dates, invitations to dances, and other pleasant social contacts multiplied. It got so that Lou was tired every day, what with running the house, working at La Golandrina, school and her burgeoning social life.

On the eve of graduation, old Burke, the Head at Westbourne called her in. 'My dear, Mrs Burke and I have been so proud of you. As you know, your tuition and allowance stopped when…mmm…when your sponsor died. I wasn't too happy letting you go to live with the Smiths. I know there are some problems…mmm…there, but they were the only family that would take both you and Joyce, so there wasn't much choice. I hope you understand. Well, I haven't said it very well, but we are very proud of the way you have helped the Smiths, and made a start at your own life. I so much wish there was a way beyond the academic honors you have earned, to show the outside world how much you have done. As it is,

Louise, we are able to graduate you summa cum laude. Now I hope that pleases you.'

It didn't really, because that meant nothing to Lou. She was headed for City College regardless of her grades, because no one had suggested that her tuition would be paid anywhere else. She needed her job, and she needed to live at the Smiths. But there was something else pressing on her mind.

'Who paid my tuition and board?'

'That's pretty direct, Louise. I'm sorry, but I don't know. Payments came from a lawyer, and that's all, truly my dear, of the facts I know.' Lou did not notice the sliding away of informed speculation that formed the head's denial.

Louise started to give up, but some anger came into her from somewhere. She remembered her mother much better than Joyce did. Her mother smelled like the Smiths, but was always loud, on the phone, or out visiting Uncle This or That, or having him at home, behind a closed door. She had only recently began to think what her mother and Uncle whatever had done behind the closed door. What with randy Junior and talk at school, she really did know. It made her mad. Why the heck was her mother so dumb? That kind of stuff only got girls pregnant. Which is probably why she and Joyce ever were born. Which made her mad at her mother, and the world in general, and at the Head that morning in particular.

'What lawyer,' she demanded, her face showing that she was against any more soft answers.

Head ruffled some papers, and finally produced Lou's folder. He carefully wrote down the address. Then he said 'Wait a moment, I have a better idea.' He pulled out a sheet of school letterhead, wrote a polite note on it, and handed the sheet to Lou. It asked Mr John Otterey of Scrivner Writhe and Otterey to give his graduating student Louise Fuller any help that he could possibly render, as this was a responsible young lady with maturity beyond her years.

Lou carried the letter around with her for several days, afraid to follow through. When Mrs Smith had an errand near the lawyer's address, she could put it off no longer. She left Mrs Smith at the dentist, and put the car in the parking lot of the law firm, a lot lavishly planted with palms and hibiscus in the manner of the parking lots of all the up-scale professionals in Santa Barbara. She presented her letter at the front desk to a carefully made-up woman who had a nametag saying Janet Read.

Janet slid her paperback under a phone directory, read the letter, looked at Lou for signs of responsibility, and buzzed Otterey's office. 'Responsibility' seemed an odd description of the determined girl standing there. Was it a compliment, or a warning, Janet wondered.

Of course Otterey could not see her. 'Probably some damn-fool research assignment from the school. A time-waster.'

Which merely confirmed Janet's opinion.

Lou would not be put off. 'I insist on seeing Mr. Otterey, and now.' She did all but stamp her foot to make herself clear.

Laughing behind the receiver, Janet, told Otterey what was going on. John Otterey was, as usual, bored, and finally allowed this weird interruption to his daydreaming. John thought that he had served enough time in the law business, and heartily wished to fish for the rest of his life, preferably without the humorless Mrs Otterey.

Bored or not, Otterey wasn't crazy enough to invite this little whirlwind into his office. He came out, waved Lou to some chairs in the waiting room, and they sat, close together in the small space. He read the Head's note, trying to remember what it was all about. Then he picked up a phone and spoke quietly to his secretary. He asked Lou some general questions about her schooling, and where she lived now. Of course he knew the Smiths. Everyone did. Or he knew enough to know that they lived a fairy tale life of wealth and that they had lots of children, all rather laid back, and with no obvious problems. He also remembered that he had never seen the Smiths without a glass in their respective hands, but that was also true of lots of Montecito people, many of whom seemed to roll from party to entertainment to party again with no obvious effect.

Janet had been thinking that old Otterey had shown more interest in this youngster than he had in anyone since he had fallen for the Gallivant widow. The intercom rang, and she relayed the message that the file Otterey sought was now on his desk. He led Janet back towards his offices, seated her, and placed himself across the desk. 'You want to know who paid your board and tuition at Westbourne, is that right? Oh, and your allowance too? Everything?'

Lou nodded, her chin still set.

'Very well. Jerry Howard paid it as long as he could. Poor Jerry was once very wealthy, you see. But he ran out of money, and there was no way he could keep on helping you. About the same time as Jerry's money ran out, his will to live seemed to go too. Poor fellow died about six months after, mmm, after he stopped paying your bill. I had to write to your headmaster. After that he called me to say that he thought he could find a way to help your sister and you. I guess I haven't thought of it since then. I'm sorry to say.'

Otterey's quiet voice seemed to allow Lou to look back into her past. She thought she remembered Jerry. Round faced, cheerful, and quick-tempered. The man who lived at the beach. In a house with a big terrace overlooking the ocean. Where she had been that night. Where something had happened. Lou returned to the present. 'Why did he help us?'

'I wouldn't like you to put anything to it, my dear. He did it, I think, because he wanted to, nothing more.'

'He never told you?'

Softly, Otterey said, 'I asked him once if you girls were his children.' Otterey spoke even more softly, 'but Jerry said you weren't, and I believed him.'

'Then whose children are we?'

'Do you remember your mother?'

Lou did, but said that her sister didn't seem to.

Otterey let her draw the conclusion for herself: father or fathers unknown.

Somehow, Lou thanked the man, and managed to get herself out of there, knowing not much she hadn't known before. But at least she had a name.

Otterey remembered considerably more than he had told. He remembered Jerry Howard waking the Ottereys at one or two in the morning. Jerry shoving one very frightened child into the arms of Mrs Otterey, and himself carrying a sleeping child into their guest room.

Jerry Howard, his client about a lease and a divorce some years before, whispered that he had just shot the girl's mother, and for God's sake to keep the girls out of it. Jerry had begged Otterey to protect the girls it being, he said, the least he could do.

Jerry had driven the dead woman's station wagon back to Fernald Point, called the police himself and been escorted to jail for booking. After twenty-four hours, Jerry had not called counsel, and the court, bemused at the folly of the rich, was about to assign a public prosecutor. John had assumed that his client had called in a criminal lawyer. When he finally visited Jerry, he was coming for instructions about the girl's immediate situation. Mrs Otterey was distinctly opposed to putting up with two sad little girls who had no table manners, clean clothes or interests beyond the television set.

Thus, when Otterey met Jerry at the County Jail, his first question was, 'What exactly do you have in mind when you said: look after the girls. Money is one part of it. Housing another, but the tough part is finding a responsible adult…'

Jerry finished it, 'To replace their mother? I guess she wasn't much, but kids need one, and I killed the one they had.'

'Jerry, don't say anything until you have counsel. I can recommend several good men, and there's no doubt in my mind that something can be worked out.' Otterey had little idea what could be worked out at that point, because he knew almost nothing besides his client's initial statement the night before: I just shot Gloria Fuller, and she's dead.

In the days that followed, Jeremiah de Wit Howard persisted in stating his guilt. A few rogue criminal lawyers scented vast wealth. Jerry did not want to see them. He insisted that a public defender be appointed, and claimed he had no wealth. But he did, although not much.

In the following weeks, Jerry was indicted by the Grand Jury, and settled in with a very competent criminal lawyer. He refused to ask for bail, saying he deserved to be where he was. The trial refused to catch the attention of the media. Who cared, after all, when an elderly rich man pled guilty, presented no defense, and was given a life sentence for manslaughter?

After the trial expenses and all his pending bills were settled, Jerry Howard's estate was down to less than a million. Carefully invested it would pay the tuition and board at the school Mrs Otterey had suggested, and something over to tuck away for the girls' college fees.

Thus, when a few years later, Jerry Howard died, he did so with the feeling that he had at least provided for the children he had orphaned. His remorse at having killed Gloria for simply saying what was true was always with him. Why the Hell, he kept asking himself, did whiskey make men so damn stupid. Sober, he might have laughed off Gloria's taunt. Drunk, he had wrecked four lives, his own being the least worthy.

But Jerry's death cut off the girl's tuition. It did so because his second ex-wife proved beyond a shadow of a doubt that he had contracted to pay her the entire residue of his estate if he died before she did. That contract superseded his will. Otterey had forgotten all about that when he drew Howard's will, and assured him that it was what he wanted. In the end, the ex got a few certificates of deposit, the inheritance and estate taxes got a tad, and the girls got zip.

When Lou came home from Otterey's office, she found Mr Smith in a garden chair looking sourly at the lawn which was uncut because the gardeners had been hired away by some free-spending neighbors. 'Stinkvogel has some more Mexicans coming in, but Holy Christ, things get out of hand the minute you turn your back. Well, what's up LouLou?'

Lou offered that Mr Vogel had done his best, but the gardeners still remembered the times when their paychecks were irregular. When Mr Smith grunted that he knew all that, Lou asked about Jerry Howard, and did the Smith's remember him.

'Sure. What ever made you think of him? Well, it's an old story. Poor Jerry loved every woman he ever saw. Most of the woman here in Montecito knew better than to fall for his line, but that still left a lot of town girls who believed him. Undying love was his line, would you believe it? I guess that sounds pretty old fashioned to you.' Smith seemed to remember that his audience was only eighteen, and said only, 'Quite a lothario was our old buddy. Poor fellow died a few years ago.' Smith leaned back and closed his eyes to show that the subject was closed. He remembered that the guy had died in jail, but he had forgotten why. Something like Richard Whitney, he supposed: financial.

Lou went upstairs, still wanting to know, and found Mrs Smith resting from her lunch-time Martinis, and talking on the telephone about an unlucky three no-trump bid which had cost her eight dollars in the last hand before lunch. Lou sat down in one of the big bedroom's many slipper chairs and waited. All the girls in the house had the privilege of the Smith's bedroom for confidences with Mrs Smith. Not that any of them gave her any, but she was most likely to go along with requests for upped allowances, toys, clothes or outings if approached here. It made her feel that she was a good mother, and in charge of things, Lou decided.

In her direct way, she asked about Jerry Howard, and Mrs Smith simply rattled away. He had been Jeremiah deWit Howard, one of the old New York vanMeter's grandchildren, and a Howard of Virginia as well. Spoiled beyond belief, but with the most infectious smile in the world. 'Made you want to step outside with him. Not that we ever did, he was just too outrageous.' She detailed his several marriages, naming the antecedents of each wife, and the causes of divorce, all infidelity as far as Lou could understand.

Mrs Smith apparently thought that everyone she knew was interesting, because it never occurred to her to ask Lou why the questions about a man who had been dead for some years. 'Eight? No, eleven or twelve. Well, dear, as you know, no one ever comes to Montecito unless they have plenty of money, but Jerry did anyway. I mean he wasn't poor, but he had to rent a house on the beach because he couldn't afford to buy one. Can you imagine?' She went on in an economic vein for a while, and came back to personalities. 'Well, he went downhill towards the end, and used to have girls from town, and took them right to the Club, if you please. That didn't go over too well, you may be sure. Not that some were not quite pretty, and nearly all were nicely dressed, but then everybody can be well dressed today. And on almost nothing.'

Lou's foot had been folded under her opposing thigh, and was getting numb, but Mrs Smith was rattling on and she didn't want to stop her. It seemed that Jerry had finally been thrown out of the Club because he was 'having it off with some member's wife in the storage room,' which was a little unclear to Lou.

She understood the next. Jerry had taken up with ever more common women, until one night during a drunken brawl he had shot his current woman.

Until she had actually spoken, Lou had forgotten…suppressed?…the sound of the shot, the yelling on the terrace, and the unseen collapse of her mother. Her mother whom she had never seen after that. And the memory of a round-faced man leaning through some bushes at her, saying, 'Don't be scared. I'll always take care of you.'

Lou started to cry, but Mrs Smith didn't notice. She was focussed on the past. 'So poor Jerry went to jail, and died there. The Parker Johnsons have that house now, and I think even they rent it. Prices have gone up so. I often wonder what we could get for this place.'

Months passed, then several years. Things didn't change much, except that all four Smith girls were away at school, and both Smith boys were running up extravagant bills for ski trips and sailing outings. Joyce and Lou stayed at home, with Joyce about to emerge from Westbourne, and asking about colleges. Both Smiths accepted that Joyce could have as much latitude as the Smith's own children in choosing schools, and both accepted that Lou, never having expressed an interest in schools, was to stay at home and take care of things. The established routine was that Lou had Vogel's complete confidence, and ran the Smith's world with a good deal more care than the long-vanished butler had, and much more economically.

In fact, Vogel initiated Lou in to the mysteries of the Smiths finances. Lots of capital, conservative investments, an ironclad trust, and intemperate spending habits. Thirty-five thousand a month coming in, and forty-nine going out. Lou could hold everything in the house in Montecito to around six thousand, but taxes and the children's expenses ate the rest. The Smiths seemed to have everything they wanted except driver's licenses and another Martini. They had reached the time of life when maintenance was costing less and less every year.

Lou realistically accepted that Jerry had killed her mother in a drunken rage. She was certain that her mother was being hard to get rid of, and Uncle Jerry had lost his temper. 'Joyce, you have to learn from our mother. She wanted the best for us, but she always picked the wrong men.' That they probably had different fathers, Lou didn't mention, nor did Joyce know anything except that they had each other, and that the Smiths were good to them, even absent-mindedly loving.

Joyce prepared to go to Dartmouth because Mr Smith had gone there, and so had Junior. She had come to her own conclusion that men were to lead, and women to follow. Junior and Mr Smith seemed like smart men, and fun besides. Lou had nothing against Dartmouth except that it was far away, which might be a sort of plus to Joyce, she acknowledged.

Lou was lonely when Joyce left, but she accepted the departure as being in Joyce's best interest. Even so, the house seemed quiet.

All this time, Lou had worked afternoons, until seven, at La Golandrina. After six years, she prepared all the sauces that would be used at night, all the dressings, and most of the deserts. She earned, now, about seventy dollars a day. Without thinking about it, the Smiths now gave Lou the same allowance as the other girls, raising it about every six months, when the six natural children talked them into it. All told, Lou could tuck about twenty-four hundred a month into the account which Mr Vogel had encouraged her to open. Periodically, he suggested mutual fund investments to her, and she herself had decided upon two stocks. IBM because that was the household computer on which her books were kept. Prentice Hall because Mr Vogel had a huge set of tax manuals in his office, and, judging by the Smiths, the world revolved around taxes, estates and trusts.

Her conclusion seemed even more reasonable when Mr Smith's sister died, leaving each Smith a nice round two million dollars. Successfully, Vogel argued that the minor Smiths should now pay their own bills, and that the Smiths should employ a daily driver, which freed Lou of several tasks a day, without, however, depriving her of the use of the aging Mercedes. This new luxury of time, Vogel suggested, should make it possible for Lou to go to Santa Barbara City College.

The Smiths were mildly surprised that Lou had not been going to University, and told Vogel 'for goodness sake, don't screw up about her tuition.' There was no tuition at City College, so Vogel suggested that in parity with Joyce, for whom there was considerable tuition, Lou be allowed an equivalent sum. The Smiths waved this off rather in the manner of royalty granting a minor favor, 'Of course. She's a nice girl, and all the girls should be treated the same, don't you agree my dear.' They agreed about nearly everything.

Joyce returned to Montecito in mid-semester, clearly pregnant. Father unknown. Not Junior, who she said would have been a shocking mate, because 'he's practically a brother.' What, Lou had inquired of Junior, had Junior been doing that his nearly-sister was sleeping around?

'Aw hell, Lou, just because you never look at guys doesn't mean that the rest of the girls don't Grow up. I'll help, lets just get her reamed out, and she'll be no worse for it.'

Lou had driven the Smiths to All Saints by the Sea every Sunday before the lunch at the Club for six years, and gone with them every Sunday before that, and at school. "I don't necessarily believe it all,' she told herself, 'but it's just common sense in pretty language. It's better to believe in commandments than in nothing, like everyone else claims they do, and that church is warm and I like going there.'

'Most things,' she told the youth pastor at church, 'I can figure out for myself.' Like refusing to let the busboy at La Golandrina feel her up when she started working there, and allowing Jimmy Sullivan, the waiter to do so. 'But this I don't know about. Abortion sounds wrong to me, and Joyce being a mother is goofy. We were sort of adopted by the Smiths, and it's been pretty good as far as that goes. They're really nice, but it's not the same as being really part of a family. 'Not,' she added feeling guilty, 'that we're not, I mean.'

Youth counselors don't often have much more experience than the youths they counsel, and Carl Werz was only as old as his twenty-seven years. 'She could let the baby out for adoption, and the agencies are really careful. I don't think there's another situation in the whole county like yours with the Smiths. Are you sure you aren't adopted? You really ought to see a lawyer about it.' Carl was thinking the Smiths were very rich, and unless these girls were actually adopted, they would be left high and dry when the Smiths died. The efficacy of the County of Santa Barbara, and therefore of its adoption agency was unquestioned by a counselor of liberal views and few years; that was the easy part of it all.

Which is why Lou returned to see Howard Otterey when she was twenty years old, blooming with an innocent color, healthy, outdoorsy, even though not a sports woman at all. Serious, but full of good humor, deferential, but with the force of character. An irresistible picture for Otterey.

He had been thinking that he hated the law and clients and suits and what he needed was about twenty years off. His telephone rang, and he said, 'Wild open spaces.'

Janet out at Reception laughed, and corrected him'

'Wide, Mr Otterey. Wide open spaces. And that Miss Louise Fuller is here again. The one that was Joyce and Louise Fuller in the Howard matter.'

When Lou finally sat in Otterey's client chair again, the older man was in love. He had half fallen for her when she was sixteen, but now, well, it was all over with him. His advice? Private placement of Joyce's baby was too risky. The County would do a better job, and yes, he would represent Joyce all the way. And, no, no fee, just costs. And some practical advice about where

Joyce might spend the next few months and get some counseling at the same time. A home for girl's in her predicament that was tucked back in a residential neighborhood in Santa Barbara. No charge, if she couldn't afford it. And then he remembered that these were the adopted children of the Humphrey Smiths of Montecito. Top drawer socially and financially; he explained what the charges would be. Lou was prepared to underwrite them, and would not pretend that Joyce was still at school, and thus entitled to money from the Smiths. She would pay it herself.

The second matter left Otterey's jaw adrift. Such generous financial arrangements seemed unreal. Yet no one had pursued actual adoption of the girls who now were as much Smiths as the other six children? This had to be looked in to.

Lou insisted that Otterey speak to no one until she agreed, but that she would bring Tom Vogel in when Otterey could see them.

When Otterey stopped as usual, at an ocean-front bar on the way home, his second drink led him, breathless, into a sort of dream world where he had married Lou, won social recognition in Montecito, and managed her share of the great fortunes of the Smiths. The fact was that, aside from a dream about fishing all day and sleeping in a sleeping bag under the stars, Otterey hated himself for being merely on the outermost fringes of Montecito society, and where his hard-earned fortune counted as nothing. Not that he had so much, but he was respectably a Montecito resident, even if his wife took a dim view of frivolous amusements. His wife. A spreading sort of woman with close cropped gray hair worn in a ducktail. She preferred long beads of an ethnic character...bones, quartzes and shells. She read serious books, and held Unitarian views. She got her news from CNN, and remembered her undergraduate days at

Columbia University with mild surprise that she could ever have been so young. A wife to be rid of, if he ever got around to it.

When Lou finally had the chance to go through it all with Vogel, his advice was clear. 'The Smiths are my clients, and they have been damn nice to you and your sister. You owe it to them to take trouble to them the same way as you take good news. Did you ever hear them mad at any of you children? Just tell them what the youth counselor said, and I'll bet they'll back you a hundred percent.'

Lou said no, we are not their children, and it's our problem, not theirs. 'And don't think you are going to them behind my back. What I told you is, um, professional, and you can't reveal what's told that way.'

Vogel laughed at Lou's idea of the confessional and the protections an accountant could not give, and gave his whole attention to the next issue. That of adoption. He was sure the Smiths assumed that Joyce and Louise were equally protected by their long practice of treating the girls as their own, and agreed that probates and the laws of inheritance wouldn't follow the Smith's assumptions. He was pretty sure he could fix it.

'Not on your life. I don't know what's right yet, and I do know that all six Smiths are spoiled and, maybe, not much use to anyone. I don't want Joyce to turn out that way, so its OK to talk to Mr Otterey, and not OK to talk to the Smiths.'

Her jaw made clear what she expected, and for the moment, Vogel agreed.

Joyce had her baby, and it was placed, ironically, with a couple from All Saints. Wertz could have put two and two together, but he was wrestling with the confessions of a confused young man who had designs on a surfer, and didn't notice the adoption coincided with the return of Joyce to the Smith's pew. Joyce was pretty teary at the christening of the adopted baby, but only Lou noticed, and cursed herself for not ruling out a Montecito adoption.

Of all the stupid things. She was going to have to watch the unknown nephew grow up without acknowledging any relationship. She had a family to whom she belonged, and at the same time was a stranger to. And she had a blood relative from whom she had to remain a stranger. It was too much. Especially as Joyce intended to transfer to the University of Maine, where the skiing was more serious than at Dartmouth, and the studies more relaxed.

Otterey was at the baptism which immediately followed the Sunday Eucharist. He made sure to greet the Smiths, and had particularly warm words for Lou, who rather liked his attention. Afterwards, at the usual Club lunch that was nearly mandatory for any Smiths who happened to be in town, Mr Smith asked if that man who flirted with her wasn't a local lawyer.

'Yes, I believe he is.'

Smith didn't ask how he knew Lou, because he was thinking how attractive she had become, and only wished it were a younger man paying attention to her.

"I think we should be introducing Lou to some younger men. Do we know any?' he asked his wife.

Which is how Lou happened to be at the Summer dance at the Club with an eddy of young people who were more interested in sneaking a drink from the private stock out on the lawn than in dancing. They wanted to get out of there early, so they could go downtown for more imaginative dancing. And how

Lou, who had no head for drinks, happened to have an unforgettable experience with a thick-shouldered blonde kid in the back of his van.

When the blonde kid called her the next day for another date, she politely thanked him for his flattery, and explained that she thought they had nothing in common. This of course inflamed the youth, who had thought that they had had an uncommonly good time together, and what else did she expect? It took all of a month for her to finally wear the eager young man out by refusals. She finally said she was in love with Jimmie Sullivan. And having said it, she finally allowed Jimmie to make love to her, ironically in the back of another van. An older but less littered van than the rich boy's Suburban.

Lou considered herself emancipated, but Jimmie expected what all the other young people expected. They were to go together, if possible live together, and be in love until something else came along.

'Sorry, Jimmie, I like you, and you have been a good friend. I liked making out with you, and maybe sometime we'll do it again. But I have my own way to go, and I don't want anyone else in it.'

Her own way still wasn't clear to her, but school was great. She wanted to be a chef. Not just the cooking part, but the managing part, the accounting, the labor relations. Everything she was learning at her culinary arts program at Santa Barbara City College. She hadn't sorted out how she got from being the Smiths' daughter-cum-butler to being an executive chef, but when she got to the point where she actually had an option...well she would know what to do.

Gin Martini's are hard on older people, as if they aren't on younger ones. The Smiths navigated the clear waters of their favorite drink pretty well, actually. They survived another pregnant daughter, one they knew about. They kept cool when Lyman went to jail for sixty days for possession. They let the Vermouth soften the blow when Junior went utterly bankrupt at twenty-six because that preserved his remainderman's interest in the family trust, even as it cost him the rest of his inheritance from his aunt. It took an extra Martini each to calm them after their youngest daughter posed for a fashion spread in Woman's Wear Daily in some see-through work shirts which made clear that she shaved no part of her body. Actually, Mrs Smith said the girl looked starved, so maybe she was not as shocked as the girl's father had been.

Anyway, family matters did nothing much to hasten the Smiths gradual decline. It was too few bites of filet mignon and squab, and too many rounds of cocktails that, almost simultaneously landed both in the hospital with symptoms of malnutrition and liver disease. They had adjoining beds, and perhaps survived a good many months because of that. In the end, they came home with two nurses and liquid diets of Ensure and other bland stuff.

'See here, young man, Mrs Smith and I always have a cocktail at six o'clock. Just you go off and ask Lou to send up a tray.'

'Young man' declined and it was several days into the homecoming when Vogel came to call. 'Now see here, Vogel, these ninnies flatly refuse to take care of us. You'll have to get some other help.' Smith glared at 'Young-Man.'

'Its always about cocktails. Everything else is swell, but they don't understand that there are no cocktails on the diet sheet.'

Young-Man had a twinkle in his eye, Vogel saw. 'Best I can do, Mr Smith, is call the doctor for you. But I think we all know the answer.'

Mrs Smith sent for Lou, and explained that the doctor's instructions were all mixed up. If Lou would kindly send a tray of cocktail things up, 'Mr Smith and I can carry on.' She waved her hand gently, her plastic hospital bracelet still in place. 'And LouLou, I'd like to wear my jade this evening.'

Lou understood. She was to take the white jade bracelet and ear rings from the safe, and keep them as a bribe for the Martini tray. She said, 'I'm so sorry Mother, but it's been so long I've forgotten how to open your cupboard.' They always said 'cupboard' so the servants wouldn't know there was a safe, although they all did, of course. 'Your dinner will be up pretty soon. I'll hurry it if you like.'

'Dinner!' the Smiths said pretty much in unison.

Vogel waited until Lou had left, and said, 'There is a serious problem here.'

The Smith's agreed, but when Vogel described the problem, it wasn't what the Smiths thought it was. The problem was that all the other Smiths had protection if the seniors died, but Joyce and Lou would be left naked by the roadside. He said it more diplomatically than that.

'Lord, that must seem mean to Lou. Joyce probably doesn't understand, but we owe so much to Lou.' Smith looked at his wife for agreement.

Still focussed on the absent Martinis, Mrs Smith had enough left over energy to say that 'Our children have gone through every penny they had from my sister-in-law, and everything else too. They're going to need everything we leave.'

Smith agreed, and turned back to Vogel.

'Then leave her the house. It's old, none of the young people will want it, and it costs a mint to keep it going.'

Anxious to get back to the main issue, the Smiths agreed. They knew the house had cost them seventy-five thousand in 1948, and had gone up in value. But houses to people like the Smiths are not capital, but sort of like permanent clothes. One has them, but one never does anything about them. It was an easy solution to a puzzling problem.

No matter how much help the Smiths had, they resisted drying out. Nor would either of them consider going down stairs again. They retired to their bedroom, and with nurses, TV and occasional visits, survived several more years. There was the nightly demand for the cocktail tray, and the regular rejection of their request. They were never without energy for the demand, and treated each six-o'clock as if it were their first request. They tried trickery.

'I'll just have some juniper juice, nothing else. Ask LouLou.' She would know that gin is sometimes flavored with juniper berries.

'Some friends are coming by at six. Have some hors d'ouvres made, and of course there should be some refreshments sent up.' But there were no guests, and everyone knew what refreshments were intended.

And, 'I wonder if they still have that old-time cough syrup. I'd like some,' Smith demonstrated a cough. 'Now what was that brand?' He worried that over for several days, because one of his nannies when he was six or seven had a glass of cough syrup every night until his parent's housekeeper reported that Annie's medicine was 25 proof. Not quite gin, but near enough.

Finally, after a wet February, Smith developed pneumonia. A tent was installed over him, and he waved gamely out of it to Mrs

Smith, who smiled gently and decided life was over. Smith survived a few days, and joined his wife.

Within months the house had been cleared, mostly by Lou's energy. Christie took the best stuff, Butterfield the next best, and local shops the rest, which was most of it. Joyce, who was living with the tallest ski instructor in Maine, insisted on having a large painting of Mrs Smith, done in her twenties. Surprised, the rest of the Smiths agreed. They had wanted nothing. Lou kept a handsome photo of the Smiths as they had been when she first met them. The photo was taken at a Club dance, and Mrs Smith looked especially well in the white jade she had tried to bribe Lou with. Of course, Martini glasses stood on the table in front of them.

The estate's assets were, in time, parceled out to the Smiths, and at the time it all seemed quite satisfactory. Mollie handled the dispersal of the jewelry, most going to Christie for auction. In her divisions, she made sure that each Smith got things of balancing value, and Lyman paid up to get his mother's big diamond for his fiancée. Mollie made sure that Joyce and Lou shared equally in the articles of jewelry, although the sales proceeds were shared out only among the Smiths. Actually, the Smiths were too busy spending and investing their money to read the list which Mollie had circulated, so no one really noticed that the Fuller girls were in the cut.

Finally, the big empty house was delivered unto Louise Fuller, an unmarried woman. Who could not pay the gardener and utilities except from her savings. Local brokers had been bugging her for the sales listing, but Vogel suggested that she rent the house for a year or so, just to see what might happen.

Otterey indicated that he would be glad to rent the house as soon as he had sold his own, but Lou couldn't wait. She moved into the chauffeur's suite above the five-car garage, and pocketed the rent checks from some people who were building a new house about ten blocks away.

Junior showed up once in a while, usually to take her to meet some new girl he had acquired. 'I don't have any sense about women. So come take a look at this one.'

Lou was tactful, always complementing him about the girl's looks, and managing to explain the likely trouble this one or that one represented. Usually monetary. Junior was known to be rich, a skillful sailor, and attractive in a non-intellectual way. Lou said she was holding out for him to settle down for a girl who had enough brains for both of them, and Junior said he'd never seen a girl with a good figure who had brains, except Lou, who'd turned him down.

Junior lived on his new boat, a forty-foot ketch, in the harbor. When he wasn't fooling around with the boat, he was trading horses and playing polo. He was athletic enough to seem pretty sound as a player, but he didn't think quite fast enough to be a good player. Pretty much his life story, Lou thought when while she watched him one day.

Carol Foy was sitting on the bleachers at the Polo Club next to Lou that day. She was a brown-haired girl with apricots under her thin tanned skin. Brown eyes. She wore a granny dresses, sandals and those slit-eyed dark glasses that make even the most pleasant expression look evil. At least she shaves her legs, Lou thought to herself.

'Your brother is the best looking guy out there, I'd say.'

'Thanks, Carol. But you are going to have to do a couple of things if you want his attention.'

Carol was outraged. 'Look, you stuck up bitch, I can have any man I want, which is a hell of a lot more than I hear about you.'

'Sorry,' Lou began, 'What I was trying to say is that you and Junior are a match if I could help you get it started.'

'Help? I don't need anything from you.' But she didn't move to another seat,

After a while, Lou said, 'Pitch the glasses first. You have beautiful eyes, but he can't see them.'

With a muttered curse, Carol yanked the glasses off. 'Next you'll tell me he can't see any T & A in this dress.'

'You have the picture.'

'Well, I won't parade around like those groupies down there, you can be sure of that.'

The groupies were polo players' hangers-on, usually tightly bundled into white jeans and silk shirts that clung to their anatomy. One girl with a deep tan wore a tan shirt unbuttoned to the navel, which the guys liked very much.

'Junior likes to think he's desirable, and makes a big thing of moving on all the girls. The truth is, I've know him for years, and he's always decent, and he worries that he doesn't meet girls as nice as his sisters.' Lou omitted that Mollie and Peggy were good sisters, and MaryAnn and Francis was the next thing to losers. But even MaryAnn and Francis looked ladylike.

The game was over, Junior's team having lost by two goals, and the riders were dismounting. The groupies and some other girls were over in the hitching area, hugging and being hugged when Lou and Carol walked up. Carol's hair was swept off her face with one of Lou's barrettes, and she had some of Lou's lipstick on. She had even unbuttoned the top two buttons of the granny dress, which made her look less shrouded. Junior included both girls with a big hug, and asked did they want to go down to the beach grill for some burgers and crazy dancing. About seven. Beers weren't mentioned because Junior ducked out whenever one of his dates took a drink.

That night, Carol strolled in wearing something light, tailored and short. But not tight. She held her hair back with a ribbon that matched her dress, and she looked about sixteen. The contest was over right then, because Junior liked exactly that look. Refined, a little dangerous, and this girl was supposed to be smart. They were married six months later. Working for a living was not Junior's problem. Carol managed his money, her money and their money well, and it was a safe bet that Junior knew when he was well off.

Lyman rolled from the correctional institute into some back-room films which he distributed. For a while, he lived on the edges of Hollywood, but a stock tip tripled the odd eight thousand-dollar stock purchase in a week. That got his attention. He went back to UCLA and pulled an MBA out of his hat. Then he joined a discount brokerage and shoved indifferent stocks at old people who should have know better. Along the line, he began to see how actually doing well for his clients gave him a happy glow at the end of the day. He cleaned up the portfolios of his clients, gave them good advice and said farewell to the shady side of the street.

'LouLou,' he said her over a weekend in her guest room, 'If I go to any of the big firms, I have to start over with cold calls. Just like a rookie. If I swipe my book from where I was, I break the ethics of my business. But a few years from now, no one will remember. I don't want to be an apprentice again.'

She told him to grow up. Starting a new book was an opportunity, not another session in grade school. This time he could begin with her, and all his Club friends and his parent's friend's kids, and all that.

Lyman finally took a desk at a top brokerage in Santa Barbara and cold-called all his school friends and their parents, and built a very fine book of old, rich clients whose stockbrokers were retiring on them. Lyman married, in time, not the debutante who kept his mother's big diamond, but a girl with a nothing figure, wispy hair and a good disposition. She said she wanted six children, which seemed right to Lyman, and they went right to work. It didn't hurt that Lou and the little mother came to be best friends.

Lou had less success helping the youngest Smith girls. Both married or lived with useless hulks who sponged on them and their friends for free sailing, skiing and trips to exotic places. About seven of these ginks passed through the lives of the two girls in three years. Finally, a large animal called Mack rolled into their lives. He had a gift for analysis, and, in an effort to salvage something out of the girl's financial wreckage, he pointed out that the house Lou had was valued in the estate at about half a million. But now it was worth double that, and how much rent did Lou get for it?

Need invented resentment. Their parents had never intended to make such a huge gift to their wards. Certainly not. She should be made to give it back.

Mollie would hear of no such thing, and Peggy didn't think it was fair. It took Junior, for once firm, to shout Mack down. Mack was several feet taller than Junior, and about as much wider, so Lou was really impressed with Junior.

The next move was a family conference. Lyman suggested that the family pool its assets, the house as well. Lyman and any other two would run the trust, and pay out the income equally to each on the basis of the amounts they had initially subscribed. Mollie had the most, then Lyman, followed by Peggy and Junior, with MaryAnn and Francis the least. Lou would be about in the middle.

This was to the obvious advantage of the two least capable of the Smiths, but Mack blustered and hollered until the two youngest Smiths refused to join. Lou said she had to think about it, and Peggy cried and said it wasn't fair, they all should have the same income, the way it was when Dad was alive.

In the end, nothing was agreed until Mack went to see Lyman with a shocking admission. He had lost half of the girls' money in something that seemed to be called Cess, Inc. Could Lyman take over before he cost the girls every thing they had left.

'I never figured out which of my sisters you are interested in. Maybe it's none of my business?'

Mack shook his head sadly, and didn't answer, which seemed to mean the he was involved with both of them. Lyman, the former porno king, closed his mind about Mack and his sisters, and initiated the required paperwork. As Mack was leaving, Lyman asked what business Mack was in.

'Trucks,' he said, 'I drive them.'

Molly, Peggy and Lou met pretty often for lunch at the Club. Mollie was as conventional as ever, and putting on some weight. She was married to a cardiologist who worked long hours, which left her free to run her house, her money and her children as she wished. Efficiently, kindly and with no particular passion. Peggy was also married to a rather uninteresting man who seemed likely to be the next Head out at Westbourne. Next Head if the Trustees could remember his name.

That was the topic one day. Mollie and Lou both thought that Peggy should be more visible in the community, and her husband should work tirelessly for some charities that this or that Trustee supported. Not the Zoo, because Peter detested animals. Not Las Positas Park because Peggy thought it was so unfair that the public didn't support it, and made all the business people carry it. Then they suggested that Peggy start being the best hostess in town. Invite celebrities, and everyone else will follow. Lou would cook for her. But no, Peter hated parties.

'That leaves: you get naked and go up there and dance on the table at the next Trustees meeting, or Peter stops leading you on about how he wants to be the next Head. Take it from me, he dosn't.'

The three women laughed, but Peggy persisted, 'Then why does he keep telling me he does.'

Mollie squeezed Peggy's hand. 'He thinks you would like to be married to someone successful, especially as you have a larger income than he does. Why don't you just tell him that you are happy the way things are?'

Mollie's problem emerged one week when Peggy couldn't join them at lunch. 'I'm falling in love with Derek Anderson. He's my personal trainer. He asked me to put some money in a gym he's building in Solvang, and he has the most divine hands. He says he likes a body that isn't all whip cord, and,' Molly smoothed her hands down her fully rounded body, 'I'm sure not whipcord.'

They laughed like teenagers, but Lou felt she had to stop this from getting out of control.

'So you're going over to Solvang three times a week for construction discussions?'

They both giggled again. But Lou made a point. 'Look, if you have to get laid by this character, go ahead and do it. That might make the itch go away. But for crying out loud, don't let Dr Doolittle know about it.' The cardiologist's name wasn't Doolittle, but Mollie thought of him that way.

Lou's turned out not to be very good advice. About a month later, Molly claimed that she was in love, and was going to leave her earnest husband and take the children to a better life in Solvang.

"How much have you loaned to Derek?' Lou was alarmed now.

After some effort to minimize, avoid and skirt the issue, Lou got a figure. 'And how much more will he need before he decides that a whipcord body suits his needs better?'

Lou was told that she didn't understand.

'Well, how's this for understand: Janie Lewis. Remember her? Derek had around a hundred thousand from her before he went back to somebody called Pinkey Bashore.'

'Pinkey is just another trainer. There's nothing between them, but,' Mollie shrugged, 'maybe before…'

'Then how come Pinkey Bashore is building a house about a mile from Derek's gym. Without a mortgage. I had it checked out.' By Victor Vogel, of course.

Mollie's eyes flickered, but she avoided the conclusion.

'The bottom line is that you have fallen into an obsession. Do you know what that is?'

The old Mollie looked back at her, suppressing a grin, 'Like Lyman watching his sick movies. He got over it.'

'Lyman had time to mess up and get over it. You have kids. They're the ones who will have to bounce back, if they can.'

'The kids never see their father as it is. They wouldn't know the difference.'

'Have you asked they if it's all right for you to move them in with muscle man? Leave school, leave their friends? Leave their father? I'd do that Mollie, unless you already know the answer.'

'But I have to have him in my life.'

'Did Mother and Dad have to have Martinis, or would they have been better off without them. Why is it that out of four girls, none of you ever drink anything? Why is it that Junior wouldn't date a girl who drank? Why does Lyman get a snoot full every time something goes wrong in his life. It's the price of his parents' obsession. Do you want to predict what screw ups you'll hand on to your kids?'

'All kids get screwed up some way or another,' Mollie wasn't buying it.

'So why add a new dimension to their problems just because you have a primitive itch?'

Mollie left, not terribly pleased with her near-sister.

Fortunately, she traced a check from Derek to Pinkey, whose real name, it turned out was Norma. The resulting shouting fit cleared the mist from Mollie's eyes. She left Solvang, driving carefully through the mountain pass, but not seeing the tumble of oaks ascending the mountainsides, and oblivious of the wheeling hawks above, and ended at the Smith family lawyer's office. Before the matter was done, she held mortgages on both the gym and Pinkey's house. Mollie wasn't to be monkeyed with when it came to money.

Mollie's husband never knew a thing about the whole matter, but he was pleased to find a good many plans were rearranged so that he could spend more time with the family, and Maggie more relaxed.

Coping with the Smiths was a breeze compared to coping with Joyce and the world's tallest skier. About the time Lou thought she had sorted out her finances and the Smiths, Joyce and her lover bounced in, stony broke.

That alone wasn't so bad, because Lou had always planned to share her inheritance with Joyce, even though there was nothing that said she had to. She just didn't want to hand any money off to Joyce, who always opened her hands to any and all who needed it. Once, she even gave her twenty dollar monthly allowance from Lou to MaryAnn Smith when the latter had fifty a week.

What was so goofy was that Joyce expected Lou to round up some money for a handicapped sports venture that would prove that all kinds of people could ski. The Tallest Skier seemed to think that he didn't really need wages if he could help all those people.

Lou concluded that selling toll booths on the Brooklyn bridge was a better charitable activity, and vetoed their idea of help from Lou, or indeed any of the rest of the Smiths. Loud anguish followed by expressions of disdain followed, and the Tallest Skier left, complaining that Joyce had led him on.

Joyce took that pretty well. 'He whined a lot,' she said. But the portrait of Mother Smith was in a storage locker in Maine, with her skis, and could Lou send for them. A long tubular box arrived in about ten days.

'Where's the frame?' Lou asked.

'We trashed it. It was icky, and Matt said it was too nouveau.'

Lou remembered the Christie's man saying of the portrait, 'Herbst had quite a run at being a society painter, and he was pretty good. But his real genius is in the frames. Just look at the art deco design on this frame. Four colors of gold leaf, laid on with perfect evenness. The different depths of the carvings make each look different, as if there were ten or even more colors of gold. I'd expect the frame to bring five, maybe seven thousand. Couple hundred for the portrait. Shall we send it?'

'No,' she had said, 'my sister will keep it.' And here it was, back in Montecito frameless.

Because Joyce had nothing much to do, she tagged along to Otterey's office one afternoon. If Otterey was smitten with Lou, he was enamored of Joyce.

'My dear, we'll have to see about you having a job. Janet is off for two weeks, why don't you come in Wednesday, and Janet can show you the ropes, then take two weeks here, and we'll see if you can't fit in one of the other offices.'

Janet did practically no work that Lou could see, and she only agreed that Joyce should take the job if they gave her some computer work, books or letters to do. This alienated Janet, who had held a stout wall against taking overflow work from accounting or the other secretaries because it interfered with her reading. But it pleased accounting, and as usual, everyone liked Joyce. They did notice that Otterey took Joyce home to the Smith's place fairly often, as it was on his way home. And Lou began to realize that Otterey was taking hours to drive twenty minutes.

'Don't get involved with Mr Otterey, Joyce. It isn't worth the mess, and he's a jillion years to old, anyway.'

Joyce said, 'I'm not,' in a resentful voice. 'We just stop somewhere on the beach, have a couple of drinks, and come on home, only I don't drink, so it's really harmless.'

Lou was, for once, without a comeback, and rather hopelessly let the matter trail until Joyce said she would be away Friday through Sunday with friends.'

Lou figured it was a man, and accused her of going off with John Otterey.

'Fat lot you'd know about it, even if I did,' which left Lou stranded in mid-lecture.

The weekend produced results which were unintended by any of them. On the Monday evening, John Otterey explained to his wife that she might keep the house, for all the good it would do her, and that he was going to run away to the woods. Near Tahoe to be exact. On the Nevada side of the lake, and damned to Mrs. O to find him.

Mrs Otterey had excellent counsel by Tuesday morning, and when Otterey drove off on that afternoon, he had no money, and no credit cards. He had, however, the willing and lovely Joyce Fuller, who had about eighteen thousand in a share-out from Lou's rental account.

Lou thought the whole thing was a disaster. The dreamers leading the dreaming, for crying out loud!

Post cards, some smoked trout (salty) and some credit card bills kept Lou sort of posted as to where the lovers had fled. For about six months, Lou enjoyed some quiet, but the fear hung over her like a cumulous. You never know what may be hiding in it.

Rather carefully, Lou accepted a charity assignment to do flowers and decorations for the Historical Museum. The Chairperson was an organizer of formidable talents, and Lou knew she could rely on the chair to make the decisions, and Lou was happy to help. She wanted no part of ego trips or hysterics. The Museum was famous for happy committees, and that's what Lou felt she could deal with.

Of course, one of the other committee members was Mrs John Otterey, who declared she would not serve with that Joyce Fuller's sister. That riot was firmly quelled by the Chair, why declared that 'bah, bah ram, bah, bah ewe, all for the clan' was the motto of any proper committee, and Mrs Otterey could just fall in with it. In actual labor for the common goal, Joyce concluded that Mrs Otterey was a tiresome and boring drudge, and Mrs Otterey decided that Lou Fuller Smith, as she was often called, was an asset to the group. Wealth and birth count, the Otterey woman concluded.

After about six months, Joyce asked if there was any more rent money to share out. She asked by collect telephone call, so Lou understood the picture. She cautiously sent some money, and, for the first time in some months, went to see Vogel.

He had always seemed firm, knowledgeable and confident before. With advancing years, he was fifty-five, what had seemed a promising career among rich Montecito people was petering out as the old rich passed into gilded retirement homes, and the heirs made their own, and egregious, mistakes with the left over big money. He was distinctly shrunken, Lou could see.

'It's not quite time to sell, Lou. The property has ten acres. There'll be another boom. It won't matter much whether your buyer gets to build two houses on the site, or ten. It's still likely to be worth two million. You really should wait.'

Lou said she was alone, and had no more resiliency. 'At thirty three, I'm worn out taking up everyone else's problems, and I just want a nice little income and a few months rest.'

'Hang in there kid, you'll be fine.'

'Vogel? You know I don't even remember you first name. Dad called you Stinkvogel, and Pestvogel you know, and I know that's not it.' She laughed at his big smile.

'Victor Vogel. Parents are an odd lot, you know.'

'Even so, dearest Victor, would you consider marrying me and loving me and caring for me?'

He would, having long worshipped Lou, and always thinking that she couldn't see him for dirt.

They were married at All Saints by the Sea with some local Smiths present, Joyce and Otterey, dressed as hippies, and a scattering of young adults from La Golandrina and the Club. During the reception in the embowered five-car garage at the Smith estate, Joyce claimed another eight-thousand dollars, because Otterey was having migraines, and she had let his health insurance lapse.

Junior professed to admire the family home, which hovered across the lawn, but was plainly surveying its value. Lyman was less obviously taking a similar survey. Only Mollie and Peggy focussed on the joy of the wedding of their nearly-sister.

Lou's apartment above the five car garage was full of Smiths and Fuller-Smiths. Below, the bays of the garage were hung with white tenting, and the floors covered in artificial turf. Some not-too-big crystal chandeliers swayed in the light breeze. Garage bays two and three held a white vinyl dance floor, and risers for a five piece combo. Bay one had the drinks table, and bays four and five held a buffet that was largely home-cooked, and staffed by caterers from the club. Outside, the driveway apron was dotted with wine barrels each planted with three white tree roses, puffs of white daisies and trailing white lantana. Traditional white draped tables and chairs filled the center of the space, and peach-colored cloths topped the tables, and complimented the bride's dress.

Everything had been done in a low key way to celebrate Lou's marriage. Mrs Smith would have approved.

The action of the evening was initiated by someone who had not been invited. News of Otterey's return, however brief, filtered from the church to Mrs Otterey's house on Humming Bird Lane. She needed no other incentive to crash the reception, and scream at John Otterey.

'You are a common drunk, and just like all the rest of the Smiths, wallowing in money and booze! You ran away with one of them just for the money, and I'm left high and dry. Well just you believe me, you old fool, you'll pay for the rest of your life for leaving me!'

His reaction was tears and he had to be led off by Joyce, who was truly frightened. 'He's not the great outdoorsman he thinks he is. Can hardly clean a fish without shuddering, and he really doesn't like sleeping bags,' she had told Lou the day before.

Now, with the babble of the reception in the background, he admitted to Joyce that he missed his old life. 'Law was a friend. I could make a good living at it, and I could dream about what

I was going to do when I retired. Now? Well, I think maybe, except being with you, it's been a mistake. Not that I don't love you, but as I say…'

'Me? You're tired of me? Think again. I'm tired of you. Sick to death of you, to be frank. So just sneak back to your earth mother, if she'll have you.'

'You don't understand anything, do you. You're so lovey lovey when everything is going all right, and the first intelligent thing anyone says to you, you close down. For God's sake, listen…'

Joyce slapped John Otterey, hurting herself more than she hurt him. He pushed her back, and she ran, crying, back to the reception. She ran, in fact, directly into Junior.

'What's up, you look like you just had a fight with some bruiser, and lost. Come on, tell your brother, babe.'

She put out her version. It wasn't maliciously tailored, but it flattered Joyce.

'I'll talk to him. No, don't worry, I'll just cool him down. Oh, do you want him back or no? '

Joyce thought about that. Tick, tick…

'Shit Joyce, you do. Back in a flash.'

Junior crossed through the party, went into the shadows where the cars were parked on the lawn, found Otterey trying to edge his Suburban between a pair of big old Canary Island date palms and a cross-parked sedan, and stood in front of him, wig-wagging.

John saw Junior suddenly looming up in his headlights. He was startled, confused and angry at the whole damn Smith lot. He meant gently to accelerate, to brush Junior aside. Instead, his foot trod heavily on the gas pedal, and before he could help himself, he had pinned Junior against the Suburban. Junior's screaming face seemed inches from John's face. Confused even more,

John reversed and again tromped too hard on the gas, ramming himself into the nearer palm tree with a party-stopping crash.

Junior, arced backwards against the side of the sedan, was still upright when the crowd surged forward. They could not see what had happened. Junior looked normal, if wild, and the headlights of the van were a safe thirty feet away. Then Junior let out a long cry of pain, raised his arms, and collapsed on the lawn like a puppet whose bars were suddenly dropped.

Joyce heard the cry, but reached Junior after others had, and was made to stand back. Frightened, she tried to stand out of the glare of the headlights, and thus, almost before anyone else had noticed, saw John, still in the van, head down over the steering wheel. The van's engine was still idling.

'That son of a bitch did it!' she yelled, pointing.

The crowd turned, but Joyce's voice also aroused John. He blinked at the wedding guests who were coming towards him. Lyman, broad-shouldered and menacing, the truly ugly bulk of Mack, and Lou, her dress billowing behind her, were headed in his direction. Fear such as a lawyer never knows in his life motivated an insane act. He shoved the van into low, and commenced to drive towards the hole in the parked cars that he had originally been turning to exit through.

That he would attempt to drive off after injuring Junior was unthinkable, and not permissible. Mack was tight, but not drunk. He had the bravery that drink provides, and stepped in front of the van, palm outstretched. Having learned from his last attempt to intimidate a pedestrian, John let the van idle towards Mack, like a game of chicken. Mack did not flinch when the inching van reached him. With almost no toe hold, and very little other than windshield wipers to hold on to, Mack leaped at the front of the van. He hung on long enough to obscure John's view of anything.

John threw in the sponge. He dropped the van into neutral.

Lyman tore the door open, and in one motion pulled John out. Holding him nearly aloft, Lyman swung a roundhouse up from the ground that had all the potential of breaking his neck. While Joyce screamed, Lou threw herself at Lyman, and broke the direction and force of Lyman's blow. She took it pretty hard on the ribs, but the moment for revenge had passed.

The wedding party now had two wounded men, and a hero. Of forty people, the three main attractions had about evenly divided claques. By the time Victor Vogel had sorted out the confusion, the Sheriff's men were there, and the medics as well. Both Deputies and Medics had seen weddings before. Knew they could get out of hand. But this was Montecito, and about the worst that ever happened was drunks and dowagers who lost jewelry. Breaker Morgan was going to kick ass until he found out what had happened.

Victor was playing it cool. 'Not much drinking, officers, just Mr Otterey got totally confused when he was trying to get his car out. The whole thing was a total accident. No, no fights of any kind.' John hoped the Smith boys would have sense enough to stick with that story.

The Medics had sedated Junior and gently splinted his legs, not to set them, but to ease the pain of motion. Lyman, seeing his brother easier now, circled back to the refreshment table, and downed two scotch whiskeys. He waited about a nanosecond, and threw back a third. By the time he got back to the cars, the ambulance men were tending to Otterey,who still sat in the van. The man looked washed out, and was indeed tranquilized as much as the Medics could calm a shock victim with a load of alcohol. He seemed to be repeating something to himself, and he was certainly smiling. A stupid smile, a meaningless smile. To Junior an infuriating smile.

'That son of a bitch is guilty of attempted manslaughter. He tried to kill my brother. You got that officers? John Otterey tried to murder my brother!'

Hearing his name through the haze, Otterey, turned, moving his legs out of the passenger seat.

The motion was enough for Lyman. The roundhouse came off the deck again, and with no one near enough to stop it, plowed right into Otterey's mid-temple. Right into the soft place between the cheek-bone and the base of the skull.

Otterey bounced off the seat, smashed his face on the front jamb of the Sheriff's vehicle, slit his nose and right eyebrow fiercely, and toppled to the ground. He landed in a fetal position, face outwards and bloody side up, empty eyed.

'Medics!' One of the Sheriff's men called, but most had registered the commotion, and all had seen most of the punch that had toppled Otterey.

'I could tell from the way he fell. It was the punch that got him.' A woman had spoken, when she would have done better to be quiet. A deputy took the woman's name.

Then the Medic leaning over Otterey called for the other three medics, leaving Junior tended only by his wife. The three medics waved the Sheriff's guys into the huddle. Vogel saw the huddle, and started towards it, Lou only inches behind him.

'Now wait, you two. There's nothing you can do.' Deputy Morgan said. We're gonna transport, but I have to say, Miss Smith, there's not much hope.'

Vogel drew Lou back to the party scene, and that seemed to draw the guests back into the drive apron. There the huge pots of roses and lantana and daisy's looked as charming as before, and smiled falsely at the Japanese lanterns, just as if the party were still going on. Inside the buffet room, the long table still showed hams, a turkey, chafing dishes of hot food, ice-sculptures of chilled food. The band played boogie, jazz and hot Latin stuff, but rather quietly; they didn't know exactly what had gone down, but no one was dancing, so it must have been pretty bad.

Two deputies were collecting names, addresses and indications of what each guest had seen. People sort of stood in line, waiting their turn before Deputy Morgan. As they left the table, they made lame excuses and farewells to Lou and Victor, and un-parked themselves carefully, and left.

By ten o'clock, Joyce was upstairs, sure that Breaker Morgan was filing murder charges against Lyman. Victor was saying that it could only be manslaughter. Downstairs, Mack nursed his tenth Vodka rocks, flanked by MaryAnn and Carol who were leaning on him for moral support, unconscious of any irony. The three caterers were packing up leftovers for the downtown soup kitchen.

The newlyweds came out of their trance when the caterer's said they were through, and not to worry about their checks right now.

'I'm calling the hospital,' Lou said, 'but I already know the answer. Junior will be doing as well as can be expected, and Otterey…'

'Then we have to see what they're doing about Lyman.'

Lou's eyes widened, 'They wouldn't arrest him, would they? I guess they have to, though.'

'I don't know, but it's sure a possibility. Anyway, he probably can get off. Especially if Lyman has more serious Junior than broken legs.'

Lou thought it was pretty stupid to talk about saving one brother at the expense of the other. She shut out the thought. It was like the damned Hershey Bar. You got one when you lost something important, and got something else in exchange. She curled up in bed, still in her peachy white dress and wept for her mother, the Smiths, Otterey, Junior and Lyman. And a little for herself.

John Otterey was dead by morning.

'Murder One,' said Deputy Morgan.'

'Nuts,' said Assistant District Attorney J. Trier Wolfe*, who inclined to the view that rich people could do little wrong for which they could not atone privately. His own wife, for example.

'This is a case of a man who was drunk, injured a friend with his car, and fell out of his own car afterwards, injuring himself.' Wolfe examined his too-long French cuffs.

'Bullshit, and you know it. Witnesses saw Lyman Smith swing on the old guy.'

'Other witnesses said Smith was merely trying to catch Otterey as he fell from the car. Unsuccessfully, but with a big swooping motion.'

'Trying to deck the old guy with a haymaker.'

'I'm presenting the thing to the Grand Jury with depositions you took at the scene.' Wolfe leaned into Breaker Morgan's air space. 'Are you prepared to say you faked your own notes? Or wrote down the wrong statements?'

Breaker held his own. 'Also I got a statement from Mrs Hollinger that Lyman hit Otterey after he fell out of the vehicle.'

'And Mrs Hollinger could see when no one else could? That would be laughed out of court.'

Deputy Morgan could see where it was all going. He folded up his belligerence to wait for a better occasion.

** He is married to GeeGee in THE WADES OF KNOLL*

Mrs Otterey, even admitting she had been deserted, now brought a civil action against Lyman. Something like the OJ case. Not criminal, the Grand Jury had ruled that no crime had occurred. Just a civil trial for her loss of Otterey's presumably ever-increasing income.

Junior counter-sued, claiming Otterey had permanently damaged him. But a pair of broken legs don't do much more than keep a man out of a track meet. As Junior was playing polo against doctors orders and common sense even before the case was heard, no one hoped for much of an off-set against Mrs Otterey's claim.

Lou tried a personal appeal. She met Mrs Otterey at the Biltmore. Neutral territory for both the old families (Lou, by association) and the Montecito wannabes like Mrs Otterey. 'But you see, there will be evidence that Mr Otterey did not want to return to his law practice, and that he was going through with the divorce, there isn't much that you lost that you hadn't already lost. So why embarrass yourself with a trial.'

The afternoon sun glistened on Mrs Otterey's trifocals. She listened carefully, but her eyes were vengeful between flashes of reflected light. 'I wouldn't lift a hand to save your sister from a scandal she created. I have nothing against you, but you are part of a family that corrupted my John. There's no getting around this.'

Apparently, however, the Otterey lawyers heard pretty much what Lou had suggested, that no matter what, Mrs Otterey was out one husband. Motions to reschedule, admit other depositions, and change judges took most of the next three years. Then Mrs Otterey fell ill, and nothing further happened until the statute of limitations ran out. Lyman got off the hook, which was damn lucky. First because he had been drinking, and second, because Joyce would have admitted, if they had asked her, that John had threatened a return to his former wife. Joyce didn't think through any of that, and Lou hadn't heard it all. Lyman had heard it, but had either forgotten it, or decided that silence was a good thing: Lyman was practical.

Victor and Lou, after such a rocky start, had a very good few years of marriage. Then Joyce met an evangelist who needed help in what he called The Grace of God movement. She made a nuisance of herself asking Lou and the Smiths for money. MaryAnn gave Joyce back the twenty dollars when reminded after twenty years, but everyone else kept their hands in their pockets.

Lou resisted her sister's pleas, and Joyce brought her evangelist back to the garage apartment for dinner. It looked quite elegant now. The brown shingle had white trim, the old hinged garage doors had given was to French doors, and the garage floor was smoothly-laid polished brick. The light in the new living room was as clear as the light in one of those Dutch paintings. The evangelist knew high style when he saw it, and he appreciated the reflection of wealth it represented. Especially among his mistress' relatives.

Pastor Forst was tall, like all of Joyce's men, lithe, dark and handsome if one overlooked his heavy brow and the gap in his too-white teeth. He bent towards whoever spoke to him, pretending that what he heard was vital to him. His congregation liked it, but Lou hated his manner. Victor said anyone who did that was faking it, and he went upstairs to his home-office in disgust. Joyce, however, was as enraptured as the Pastor's congregation.

'So, can we give you the Grace of God?' Forst concluded a long oration with the invitation to contribute in return for what he called the Grace of God.

Lou offered more coffee.

The pastor tried again. 'God's Grace can not be offered again, my dear,' he said pushing his luck.

'Look here, Joyce may have forgotten, but I have been every Sunday for twenty years to our little church down there,' she pointed,' and I get all the Grace I need from that service and those simple beliefs.'

With renewed hope, Forst said, 'Ah, you are a fundamentalist. Good…'

'No. It's called Episcopalian. We only have to share ninety seven words of agreement. That's fundamental. All the rest of how and what we believe is up to us. I don't need anything else, and I'd rather support my own church. Sorry.'

'But this is a new God-be-Withness, never shown before. I'm sure…'

Lou interrupted again. 'Why make something new when I already have what I want. You're just playing with your own ego, Forst. Or is this about money?'

Joyce rebelled, screaming that dear Buckey hadn't had a choice. She hauled her lover outside, aiming a few parting remarks at a now contrite Lou.

She should have been more diplomatic. After all, swindler or scoundrel, he was a man of the cloth. Which proved to be dead wrong.

First, Furst secretly had the sister's property appraised. If Lou had not been alert to what was going on at the Smiths, she would never have seen the man measuring and photographing the grounds and house, and second, would never have had his card. And the name of the appraiser's client. Grace of God Church, the man said.

Lou went in at once and called Joyce, who was out. And apparently stayed out for days. No Joyce, no Grace of God headquarters, no Forst in the phone directory.

Victor had property records checked. No dice.

About a week later, Lou was sued. Grounds? Sequestering Joyce Fuller's inheritance, believed to be as much as five million dollars.

Victor and Joyce laughed. Between them, they intended that Joyce share in Lou's inheritance and the accumulating rent. Smith Farm seemed to be worth as much as three million. There was about sixty thousand in the rental account. Five million was a joke. Either a trust had to be created to protect Joyce, or they had to hand money to Joyce in measured amounts: a dose for each problem. They would fight this claim, probably by Forst, rather than Joyce.

Lou's investment capital, which had grown a lot, but came mostly from her old savings, she intended to keep. Joyce had saved nothing, and quite unemotionally, Lou had no intention of rewarding Joyce for being too generous.

Joyce's address was listed in care of a Ventura lawyer, twenty miles down the coast. They had never thought to check the Ventura phone directories, but Ventura made perfect sense as a place for a new church. It had a young population and lots of innocent people.

Lou cast a regretful thought towards John Otterey. When they had first met, he was a real help. Kind and resourceful. Now, they consulted the Smith family law firm. August practitioners of estate, trust and property law. Mr Phillips' first question: Did you ever tell your sister that you were sharing your inheritance with her? Second: Did you ever tell anyone else, Smiths or other, that you were taking the property for a share-out with your sister.

She had told her husband.

Had he told anyone, or mentioned it in passing?

He said not.

'Finally, did Mr or Mrs Smith ever say they wanted the property to take care of both Fuller girls?

Both Vogels said no.

'Why not?'

'Joyce wasted every cent she ever got her hands on. She's the softest touch in the family. The Smiths knew it, and so do, sorry to say, all the drifters and bums in town.' Victor shook his head sadly. 'She doesn't pay any attention to money. Has no interest in money.'

'Well, she must have some interest. This suit is about money.' Phillips concluded the interview.

Back at the Smiths, Victor and Lou discussed the problem. Should they settle with Joyce, and let her waste the money? How about a trust for her share, so she can only use the income? Probably impossible to prevent her breaking into principal for her needs, even as she gave the income away. Maybe she'd break up with Forst? See through him. That had happened before.

'Should I talk to Lyman and Mollie about it? They have awfully good sense.'

'I don't think so. Lyman has hinted that this property is worth a whale of a lot of money now. Maybe three million. He's pretty fair, but some of that would be good for three of his sisters, you know. And Junior? I know he admires you, but it's a lot of money, like I said.'

The Vogels worried these ideas on a regular basis, while the law suit lay heavy on them.

Joyce and Buckey Forst got on like tops as long as Forst ministered his brand of unctuous religiosity, but when he bought himself a gold and diamond Rolex, Joyce had a fit.

'That money was for the ministry! How could you?'

'We raise money by being attractive. We show people that God graces those who serve him. My people understand, and so should you.'

Joyce bought that, and helped as before. She mopped the hall, cleaned the dishes, mashed huge loads of instant potatoes, and cleaned the grease vats with equal fervor. Then Pastor Forst upgraded his Buick to a Jaguar. Joyce cried out at the sin of vainglory.

Forst roared, 'Where did you get that morsel, dearest? Not from me. You going to the competition behind my back?'

Joyce hated being made fun of, and began to watch how Buckey Forst handled his money. It wasn't other women, he was too regularly with her to manage anything else. But expensive pens, a second watch, a new snakeskin briefcase from Mark Cross appeared. Then a quite nice diamond ring for her, and an unconditional offer of marriage. That seemed more reasonable to Joyce.

Buckey pretended disinterest in her law suit, although of course he had started it. First, he had Joyce pray with him for guidance. Then, when she had no message from God, he shuddered, threw back his head, and drank in God's direct word.

"Tell me, dear, what did you get?'

'Revelation! A bolt of thought like a golden shower.'

'Do you know what it means?'

'Yes, my dearest one, it means that we are to use your money for God's work! For The Grace of God. Oh, thank you dear Joyce for making it possible!'

Shortly after that, they filed the law suit. Of course, Buckey already had the appraisal, which proved that the suit was worth while. He never mentioned it to her. But the appraisal, at four-point-five million was interesting, consuming, in fact. Not that she knew of it. Joyce missed her sister, but only when she wasn't caught up in work for the benefit of Grace of God. Sometimes she thought of calling Lou, just to chat. Twice, she did, and the love of the sisters carried it through without a hitch.

Joyce felt a little disloyal towards Buckey Forst because she questioned the way he raised money and then spent it on himself. She said nothing, and waited for understanding.

One wet winter day, Buckey came back to their apartment to tell her that they would be moving up the hill. He had bought a house. He called it a Manse. 'Suitable for entertaining the elders and donors. Like your house in Montecito, only new. You'll like it.'

His description frightened Joyce. How could he take those poor people's money to buy a big house to live in! But she knew if she complained, he would ask her to 'Cry out to the Lord to save us,' which meant she'd have welts on her haunches for weeks. He made love very well afterwards, and at first that hadn't been so bad. But 'Crying out to the Lord' hurt, and she was tired of it. God, she began to think, could be reached in more ordinary ways. At least that's what most of the worshipers believed.

The next day, they went to the house in the whisper quiet of the Jaguar, to be met by a broker with a toupee and diamond ring. 'Not every day I am privileged to sell to my Pastor,' he said.

Joyce had never seen this man in the congregation. The wig would frighten the children, she thought.

'Yes, my dear, this is Mr. Buncle, who is our new director of Real Estate Acquisitions. Mr Buncle has just contributed his commission to help us purchase the Manse.' Forst bowed his head for a second, and marched Joyce in through leaded glass double doors.

She hadn't seen much of the outside of the house. It was new, just landscaped and raw looking compared to houses she knew in Montecito. The living room spread before them, all yellow varnished oak floors. Some extra low couches were placed at angles to the walls, and a huge low table mounted on tree branches was centered meaninglessly in the middle of the room. Very bright cotton copies of oriental rugs lay this way and that on the floors. The walls stretched up to a high cottage cheese-coated ceiling which sloped in several directions. The windows were ceiling high, as if they were meant to follow the pitch of the roof, but oddly half-rounded just where they should have kept the diagonal. A restless space. Especially as the windows framed only the fence of the back yard.

He said, 'Seeing your sister's place, I know you can make a cozy nest here for our flock.'

Joyce realized he meant it. She had no interest in tasteful interiors, but she realized he was unable to see where this shiny new-built barn couldn't touch the effortless chic of Lou's converted garage. And this was a goofy space for plain-truth Christians. It looked more like a Praise the Lord set than a devotional reception room. She squeezed her eyes shut against it.

Pastor Forst was boasting about the convenience of the kitchen, and the camaraderie the sweep of the rooms would give.

Lou squeezed her ears shut.

In the end, they moved in a few days later. Buncle had produced some discount furniture, including a pair of plaster loins, gilded to a glow-in-the-dark finish. 'God's Guardians,' Buncle said as they were deposited on the porch steps, facing each other, perpetually snarling, instead of facing out, to protect the household. That's the way it was in the house. With no money, and no skills at this sort of thing, Joyce just couldn't produce the Montecito effect that Buckey seemed to want.

Tempers flared. Buckey spoke of the need to Cry-Out-to-God, and Joyce began to look for some way out.

One Monday a pile of mail arrived, together with copies of a mortgage guarantee that Joyce had not made, but which seemed to be signed by her. 'How could my signature be that important, that you would sign my name without my saying so?' Joyce was more hurt than angry.

Forst calmed her down, but she understood, at last, that the value of her interest in the Smith home place was behind the purchase of this house. Some local thrift institution had failed to understand the law suit. Or had they? Was there more there than Joyce had thought. She called Lou, and spilled the beans. 'So how can he need my guarantee of a loan for three hundred-fifty thousand. Is my share of your place worth that?'

'Dear, it doesn't matter. What matters is that Pastor Forst has set you up. I think you should come up here for a few days, and let's sort this out. Will you?'

Joyce was afraid to go, and let it show when her husband came home. Buckey demanded a Cry-Out-to-God session. That frightened Joyce as much, but she endured it. The next morning, still sore, and full of Advil, Joyce put Clorox in Buckey's sugary coffee. As usual, he bolted his food, sloshed it down with coffee, and got a horrible reaction of burns, bad taste, and vomiting. Contrite, Joyce called 911. During his convulsions, Buckey called her a rich whore. And a few seconds later, said that God hated her. Both seemed untrue to Joyce, and his pain frightened her even more than the accusations. She picked up the cast iron stew pot he insisted in having his oatmeal cooked in, and with fair strength, bonked him on the head. When the Paramedics rushed in a while later, Joyce was eating a Hershey bar. Her own little reward for dealing with her problem.

The morning was a terrible confusion. Lou took the call from the Ventura policeman, who put Joyce on the phone. When she finally understood what was happening, and that Joyce was calmly saying that she had done it, she ended the call in tears. Then she called Victor, who said he would round up the best lawyer he could, and let her know. Meanwhile, Lou should keep cool, and he would come to take her down to Ventura as soon as he made some calls.

Lou couldn't wait. She called Mollie, who came over immediately, bundled her into the car, and drove her to Ventura. On the way down, Lou kept repeating that Pastor Forst had driven Joyce crazy, and that she wasn't responsible. 'We'll get people who saw what was happening.' Lou also said it was her fault for not keeping a better eye on her sister. 'She's always so trusting!'

Joyce was still at the garish Manse when Lou and Mollie got there, but she had been sedated. The police doctor said she had been too calm! A policewoman told them they could see Joyce, but not to expect to talk to her.

Lou asked the police to secure the church records, and been told, 'Everything in good time, lady.'

Around noon, Lou heard that Victor was on his way, so she left to go to the church, or whatever Buckey Forst had called it. 'That's the kind of thing that falls apart the minute the guru turns his back,' she told Victor. 'I'm getting names and addresses before some one walks off with them. Mollie agrees. That bastard drove her to this.'

God's Director of Real Estate, who had houses for sale near the Manse, had seen the police cars, asked the key question, had hightailed it for the church. He too figured that records could be worth something.

Lou borrowed Mollie's car, and went in search of The Gathering Place. When she finally found it, some man was stuffing file boxes into his car. She wasn't having that, so she drove Mollie's Lexus, a nice green one, to a point where it blocked the drive out of the parking lot, and demanded to know where he thought he was taking the boxes.

'No lady, it's none of your concern. I'm the Director here, and who are you?' He smiled and wiped his brow carefully, so as not to disturb the toupee.

'You better take all those boxes right back into the office. The police want them.'

'My name's Bunkle, mam,' he had taken in the size of her ring, the value of her car, and the assurance wealth brings. 'I'm just protecting these records,' he hesitated, 'The next Pastor is going to need them.' If he had the nerve, he hoped that would be himself. 'So excuse me, these are Grace of God records, not poor Pastor Forst's.'

The argument ended when a police car stopped beyond Mollie's convertible. In the ensuing excitement, Lou carefully ranged her self on the side that favored Bunkle because the police showed no disposition to allow Bunkle to cart anything away. If she and Bunkle could be allies on this, maybe she could get some dirt on Forst from the man who seemed to think he should be God's next assistant.

When the files had been returned to the office, an officer put yellow tape on the doors: POLICE NO ENTRY. Bunkle acted like he went along with that.

Later, at a coffee shop, Lou told Bunkle that he seemed a good sort, and she would like to help him, if she could, and could he tell her about the church.

Cautious at first, Bunkle soon sold himself on his great prospects. He slid into the assumption that the great estate that Joyce shared would still be available to the Grace of God, because Joyce would want it so.

'Of course, you understand I don't know my sister's intentions. And I don't really know how this is all going to come out about Pastor Forst's death. But how can the church need so much money? Don't the members give enough?'

'Pastor Forst used to say you can't grow without looking successful. It's that way in my real estate business. I have to have a Cadillac, nice clothes, and self-assurance, or people won't buy.'

Lou nodded. The principal was sound, but the man across the table didn't know that his Cadillac was dented and scratched, and, even empty of church files, littered with papers and soft drink cans. His suit was puckered at the seams and black to boot, and his self-assurance seemed to go and come.

Thinking that he had sounded too materialistic for the next Director of Grace of God, he corrected himself, 'Not that Pastor Forst ever said it like I did. I just translated his thought into layman's language, you understand.'

Lou expressed gratitude for his clarity. 'But how would the money be used?'

'Well, there wasn't much money on hand, so we started with a house, because it could be managed. Later on, we will get a place of Gathering.' His hands sketched a steeple.

Lou pictured the alliterative sign out front: praying hands framing neon letters, 'Gathering of the Group for Grace of God.' She had to take up her coffee to hide her giggle. 'You must be pretty skilful to buy that house without much money.'

Bunkle looked at the bait, thought that it couldn't hurt to brag because this rich woman...the diamond, close up, was a stunner...would help him. 'We had five percent to put down. My commission went in, and Mrs Forst's guarantee did the rest.'

Knowing the answer, she asked anyway. 'The house is in my sister's name?'

'No, in Grace of God.'

'And when did Joyce sign the guarantee?'

'Don't know. When the lender said they needed it, Pastor Forst took it home, she signed it, and he brought it back the same day. Nice lady, your sister.'

'So you saw Joyce sign the guarantee?' She kept her voice soft.

He shrugged. 'Course not. Like I said, he took it to her, and brought it back. I stayed at the office, and didn't actually see him take it back. Very nice of your sister.'

Lou thought some good had been done. She could prove that her sister's name had been forged. Besides, she had a church insider who saw that his economic interest was best served to keep Joyce friendly, and, more important, innocent.

Lou went back to the Manse as soon as she could get away from Bunkle, because Mollie would need to go home. She found that the police were allowing Joyce to rest. The lawyer would meet them at the house the next morning. Victor and Lou decided to camp there for the night, even though only Lou's room and the living room were really furnished. Mollie went home to her, she asserted, starving children.

In the morning, Lou and Victor met Gunnar Hegstrom. The lawyer was a young blonde with the sunburned air of a surfer, and hair that flopped on either side of his friendly face like the ears of a particularly happy spaniel. Lou understood why he worked magic with jurors: who could disbelieve him? And by extension, how could he have a guilty client.

Joyce, a little unsteady on her feet, joined them. She looked rested, and her conscience was right on the surface. As soon as she understood who Gunner was, she said, 'I hit the son-of-a-bitch. He'd been cheating all those nice people, and I finally figured out he was as dishonest as they come.' For good measure, she added, 'I am such a chump!'

Lou tried to reassure her that she was not, but Gunner jumped in.

'Joyce, that's a better defense than that he mistreated you, if he did.'

That set off a round of sobbing, Gunnar asked a few questions about whether Forst was violent with her, which she denied.

Lou said very gently, 'That's not true. He did something you told me you couldn't stand. Tell me, and don't even think about being embarrassed.'

Joyce said it several times before they got what a Cry-Out-to-God meant. Being tied, being beaten, being raped, and then beaten again until the victim cried out to God in exactly the words Forst dictated, which were different every time.'

Victor said 'Ugh,' when he finally understood, Gunnar stopped looking happy, Joyce cried, and Lou stood up.

'Other woman have had this experience? Who?'

'Maybe not in this Group, but maybe in the ministry where he came from…' Lou's voice trailed off.

Gunnar said to hold the detective stuff and the lawyer ideas. To wait until he really understood what had happened, and took Joyce through the morning of the day before.

When Gunnar was satisfied, he summed up for them. 'Manslaughter is a crime without intent. If she did not intend to hurt the man, and acted out of momentary fear, or some other strong immediate emotion, we have a defense. Joyce acted in fear. That's our first defense. She had been led into a situation rife with fraud by a man she found was not the good and Christian man she thought he was, her name had been forged, and she faced another cruel punishment for asking him to be honest.'

'We're not Christians,' Joyce said.

'What? It's all Bible teaching, isn't it?'

'No, it's God's teaching of the prophets. Christ was just another prophet with a cult attached to him. The opposite of what God would have wanted.'

Angry, Lou asked, 'And who decides what God wants? Jerks like Buckey Forst?'

Joyce took refuge in more tears. 'I believed him! It is so pure, so basic!'

Victor and Gunnar traded glances, then Gunnar asked, 'Could I arrange a defense in which we never describe whether we are Christian or not? I mean unless someone asks you directly? Just you promise you won't correct anyone who calls you a Christian again. Can you do that?'

'Pretend, you mean?'

'Look, I want to get these charges modified, dropped, and made null. Juries don't like what you said, so in your own interest, just don't explain what you believe in unless there's no other way to answer a question.'

Gunnar left the room, headed for the kitchen.

Silence prevailed because Lou had given a nix sign to Victor. She knew Joyce. She would understand Gunnar's warning, if she had some quiet to think about it.

When Forst came back, he said, 'I called the police, and said you would like to come down and make a statement about all this. Was I right?'

Joyce nodded, they finished dressing, and left together.

The days passed, the police had been sympathetic, the Ventura District Attorney had been polite, and they had to wait for the Grand Jury to hear the facts, and decide whether to charge her or not. Junior brought his boat down to Ventura and took Joyce for a sail. He, like all the Smiths, wanted to cheer her up. Even Mack, with MaryAnn and Frances on his arms, tried to bring cheer to Joyce.

Joyce was coming from a funny place, they all discovered. She insisted in living in the Manse because, 'I promised to pay back the loan, and I might as well use the place while I do.' She had Mrs Smith's portrait sent down, she unrolled it, and glued it to the over mantel with starch. 'It will just peel off when I decide what kind of frame I want.'

The first Sunday after Pastor Forst's death was busy at the Gathering Place. Bunkle and some other men preached re-runs of Bunkey's old speeches, a thin collection was taken up, and a few people stood to praise the departed. Joyce had been sitting in her simple black dress, rather alone in the first row. She had been firm that Lou and Victor were to stay in the back row.

The Group had not known what to make of her. They'd come hoping to see a real murderess, and might have been inclined to turn their noses up if she didn't show all the right moves.

Joyce had no idea what the right moves were. Before another member could start a memorial speech, Joyce got up. Her voice was quite firm. 'I am a fallen woman. I have broken Commandments, and I have to tell you about it, and what I will do to keep God's work going on.'

She said she had the Manse because Pastor Forst had signed her name to the loan papers. That had hurt her very much when he did that without her consent. It had hurt her very much when he had said that the Group was just cows walking along to the slaughter. Cash cows, and that he loved them for that.

The room half believed her, and half reviled her for dishing her late husband. The racket was huge and unreal as husbands disagreed with wives, or whole families choose sides.

'Wait. Wait! I'm telling you what I'm going to do about this.'

Curiosity got the better of wanting to be on the winning side, whichever one that was.

'Thank you. Please listen carefully, so we leave here in God's Grace.

'What my husband preached was the word of God. You heard him, you know that he spoke truth. His own personal life? Not perfect, in fact like the humans we all are. I'll pay for my house, and together we carry the Gathering Place. But no pay for ministers. We gather, we say what God put in our mouths to say, we read the Prophets of old, as we were taught to by our late pastor…but no one is head. We are all heads together. Those who must leave, do so in the Grace of God. Those who stay in our Gathering will walk in the Grace of God. I feel his great peace…' She bowed her head, and all those present did the same, Lou included.

This was so unlike Joyce. It was as if that crook had turned her into someone confident, gifted in oration, and indeed, within the Grace of God.

The meeting ended with an affirmation of support that appeared to be unanimous. Joyce made no effort to be in a receiving line, but that's what it came to be. Member after member came by, kissing, hugging, and promising support. Joyce accepted it all humbly, and while Lou and Victor stayed well away from her, they could see her confidence building. When almost everyone had left, two women went to her, and, in the now-quiet room, Lou heard one ask, 'Did he ask you to Cry-Out-for-God?'

Lou yearned for Joyce to get confessions from the women, to make them bear witness in Court for her. Victor had to hold Lou back from interfering.

Glancing towards her sister and Victor, Joyce soothed the women, and they heard one say, 'Was it really his way of teaching us to speak to God? Or his bad side?'

Looking directly at Lou, Joyce said in a small voice that carried easily. 'I think it was his hope that God would hear, but I think he didn't really have it right.' And lower, 'Why don't we forget about it. He did so much else right.'

To Lou's surprise, the women nodded, and arms around each other, left.

The Grand Jury refused to charge Joyce. Lou revised her financial planning. She took out a million dollar mortgage on the Smith property, put half in trust for Joyce, and immediately started paying half of each month's net rent to Joyce. That provided for all of Joyce's present needs.

Then they put the Smith house on the market. Within weeks a buyer had appeared. For the huge sum of five-point-five million, subject only to getting eight water meters so the place could be subdivided.

Typically, Montecito, which is not a town, but a part of the County of Santa Barbara, was having a water shortage, and the County declined to issue more than two more meters to the Smith property. Even before the Smith's owned the property, there were two water meters. One for the orchard at agricultural rates, and one for the house and garage. Victor thought that would blow the deal, and said so.

Then a large family with a new electronics fortune offered to buy the main house and five acres. Victor said they should hold that one until they had an offer for the other five acres. They didn't have to wait long.

The very thin, very politically correct wife* of the producer-writer of the hugely successful TV series Pure Passion wanted the site. 'I'll tear down that garage building, it's just too twee,'

* *She was Caroline Woods who appears in TAX DODGE*

the woman said, and unrolled plans for a glass cube to be built in the exact middle of the site. Lou cringed, but in the end she took the money anyway. But she had the mounting block jacked up onto a pallet, to be moved with them.

The Smith children, oblivious to anything as mundane as real estate transactions, were outraged when they heard the price Lou had gotten. Friendships and affections nurtured after twenty-five years were strained, pulled and faltered. Suits were threatened, but the children's long acceptance of the status of the Smith property made a half-dozen lawyers tell the Smiths to pack it in. They were too late to assert any rights, if there even were any.

Lou, astonished at the reactions of those she thought of as family, couldn't understand it. Each Smith was at least twice as rich as she or Joyce, and some, like Lyman and Mollie about ten times richer.

She and Victor packed for their move up the coast to Knoll, a little community along the beach. When it was almost done, Fed Ex brought a package from Joyce. A dozen big Hershey bars. Every time you loose something very dear, something else comes along. Victor said, 'For crying out loud, that Joyce is an odd one.'

Lou simply sat on the old mounting block on which was carved 'Smith Farms,' and stuffed the chocolate into her mouth and cried.

THE END

The Day the Dogs Took Over

THE DAY THE DOGS TOOK OVER
A Cautionary Story

What I'm trying to write down is when Mom and Dad went to LA and haven't ever come back. Estella came in that night to do dinner, and she said they must have got caught in the ry-ot in LA that was on TV. We watched it for a while, but it was all people shooting each other, and cars crashing on the Freeway, and she said we better turn it off. The lights went out before she could do that, and she stayed all night so I wouldn't be alone in the house.

The dogs took over running everything about then. The day or maybe more after Mom and Dad didn't come back. Yin had to sleep with me, and Yang had his big wet face in mine all the time. There was no time to do anything with them hanging around and whining and bringing the leashes all the time. All the time they wanted to eat. That was OK, so did I. But after Estella went home, there was only two cases of dog food, and about the same amount of canned stuff for me to eat. The freezer was full, as usual.

One morning the pool guy came, and he said there was stuff going on downtown Santa Barbara, and the liquor store in Montesito village was loo-ted. He said we should be safe in here, as long as we kept the gate shut. The electricity was on again, so he came in and went out just fine with his clicker. Estella went to her house, and brought back some more food, and she stayed about two days. Every night it was the same on TV, until the President came on and said it had to stop, and they started showing old movies, and there wasn't anything more about LA or ry-ots. Estella said there was ry-oting all over all the other citys in the US, and she got really scared. As if I wasn't?

She said she had to go home and see to things, and not to worry she would be back with her daughter because our house was safer than her house. I guess she meant to bring her daughter and her boyfriend and their kid, but she never did, and maybe she went back to Mexico.

Nobody came around after that, but some kids trashed a house across our street, and got bombed out of there skulls, and set some fires. There was gunshots all around, but no one came close to our place. The dogs cried, and I had to spend most of the time feeding them and walking them around the yard on leashes. They kept bringing the leashes to me, and that was what they wanted. They burned a big hole in my time, because I had good computer games, and it takes time to make dinner and wash stuff up.

The pool guy came with some girls and said he was driving to the mountains, and I should come. Mom and Dad were still in LA. I hope. So said I better stay right here so they can come for me. He left his clicker for me. That day, I used the clicker and opened the driveway gate, but the street was empty, and it scared me. So we went out the back, way, down the wash, and through the tunnel under the freeway to the beach. Yin and Yang were all excited at going to the beach again. Labs really like water. We came out kind of up the way from the Miramar

Hotel. There were a bunch of older kids down at the Miramar, and they looked like they were having some kind of fight. There was also a bunch of dogs running around, half fighting, and partly playing. Yin and Yang sort of wanted to go check the other dogs out, and they wanted to go in the ocean if I would go too. So we did, but we had to stay there until the other dogs gave up trying to get us into there game. My dogs wanted there leashes on right now, and wanted to go back up the creek to our house.

I guess we never tried the gate again, and we were glad to stay home. The gardener never came at all, so from the outside, our hedges were really tall, and hid the house even from across the street. Dad said our house was the garages and servants 1/4s of the big house next door, the Dorch family. So from the street, it all looked like part of the same place.

I guess I had forgotten about neighbors, so I parked the dogs in there run, and shinneyed over the wall into Mrs. Dorsch's yard, and went up to the back door. It was busted in, and inside was a big mess. I looked around, and finally at the garage. Her Jaguar was gone, so I guess she left. Whoever got in there broke lots of stuff, but I guess they didn't know about living in Montesito. They didn't even try to get into the larder, which is a big old closet in old houses like Mrs. Dorsch's, so I snagged the key from the rack behind the swing door, and filled a basket, and locked the place up again. It wasn't stealing, and she was always pretty friendly, and Mom could pay her back when she got home.

That night the electricity went off pretty much for good. I had been making freezer food petty much, and feeding me and the dogs, and used stuff. Well, after a day or 2 the freezer food was pretty smelly. At camp they said you got tomain that way, so I halled it all out, and the dogs ate some, and I berryed some.

I broke the hand can opener, so I went back to Mrs. Dorsch, and borrowed hers. More kids had been in the house, trashing things. But they never found any larder stuff, but the frig was open and stinking. That day the place smelled like distilled, so I guess that's why they came. Bombed out of there skulls, I guess.

Dad said that when some guy came over in a blue suit, and made drinks out of the bottles that said distilled. He ranted and raved about his job and his corporate culture, and Dad just let him do it. Pretty soon, he broke something on one of Mom's little tables, and they made him go to bed, where he was sick and barfing and kept me awake. The next day, Dad made a big explanation about being bomed out of his skull, and it was stupid and just like Tom-whatever, but it is better to help a friend in trouble than turn him away.

So these gangs of kids were in trouble all over the neighborhood houses, and bomed out of there skulls. I don't know where the parents are, as if all parents went away at once, and just kids were left. I wish they would come back. Everythings a mess, and I don't know what to do. Staying inside our walls is safe, like the pool guy said, but if it wasn't for the dogs keeping me busy, I would be a nut case.

I wrote the above some years ago, when I was a kid. Now, I am five years older, so am a man. It has been a bad time. There isn't anyone around. Sometimes I can hear drunks breaking up something they haven't already trashed. Two of the houses on our street burned down, and last year there was a humungous fire that burned about everything up on the hills. And the house on the other side, not Dorsches. She has a tile roof and so do we.

Of course I ate everything the gangs didn't get at Dorsches. Funny, they cleaned out her bar, but left all the cans of peanuts and mixed nuts, which came in very handy. Then I started checking the other houses around, and the ones on the back side of the wash. Early in the AM, the kids are too drunk to pay any attention, and I don't go out in the street. There is no electricity so I can't get out that side, just over the chain fence into the wash.

I tried the house most nearly opposite us first, and that was bad. The old people who lived there just went in their bed room and shot each other, and they were there about a year before I checked the place out. The gangs had been there, swiped the liquor, and missed lots of canned food, and all the bar snacks. But it was all I could manage to carry the loads home. I hate that house.

Up the block some people named Temple have a big library. So I have borrowed a ton of books, because I have read all of ours about twice. The Temples didn't have much food around that was left, but a case of dog food and some cat food were appreciated by Yin and Yang. There is no water at the Temples house, so I wonder how long ours will last.

Last night it started to rain. When that happens, the wash behind our house fills up, and all the yard clippings wash down. If the Division of Highways doesn't clear the drain under the Freeway, the branches and cuttings make a dam and flood the freeway. That happened when I was a kid and Mom and Dad were still home. When the tunnel clogged up, the water off the mountains made practically a lake, and flooded some houses down that way. We even had water almost up to our lawn in the back.

This morning there is no more Division of Highways. In fact there hasn't been a car on the Freeway as long as I can remember. Almost since the pool guy left. So I went down to see what was happening, and the same old thing. A lake was damned up behind the tunnel, water and dirt were already across the Freeway, and the water was building up in the creek behind our house. And it is still raining.

When I cut behind the Dorsches house, I heard some crying, and there was a girl. She was a mess. There weren't any gang kids around that I could see, so I took a chance and brought her home. She said she had a hangover, and couldn't climb the fence, but I got her over anyway. Yang made a fuss like it was Christmas, but Yin has been too sick to care, and didn't even come outside to see what Yang was carrying on about.

So now I have three crazies who are in charge. All three are hungry all the time, and all three want to be told that everything is going to be all right, and Good God, I don't even know. So I act calm, and praise them, and say things I don't know anything about to get them peaceful again. Then they are hungry, then I feed them, and it starts all over again.

Anyway it's a good thing we have bananas. Dad used to say we live in the Banana Belt of Montecito. Which we do, because we have three kinds of bananas in our yard, and oranges and grapefruit and about as many little tomatoes as I can eat. Even the dogs eat bananas. And avocados. Two kinds. But we miss the canned food, because it was so interesting. So many kinds, and all tasted good when we warmed them up.

We still have gas and water, so we're pretty comfortable.

Yang died, great big brute. He was on our bed as usual. He looked at me, made a sort of pant, and died. Took me all day to wrap him in a blanket and get his place dug out, down by the creek where I put Yin, alongside the cat we buried when Mom and Dad were still here. I'm really down because he was the last thing that was alive when my parents were at home, and we lived the way people do in books. That made me decide to write all this down, taking up where I was when I was fifteen and brought Kim home.

Kim was so dirty I made her have a bath in Mom's tub, and made her wear Mom's bathrobe. She didn't want to wash her own clothes, so I let her wear Mom's, which were mostly too big. Kim was about thirteen she thought, and ready as a rabbit. She'd been doing it for about a year then, and I was a rank amateur, so she taught me, and it is a great thing. Makes you feel free and grown up, and happy all at once. But it makes Kim sad, and all the time going into tears about where are we, and what to do, and when will we ever go out and see the other kids.

That's a problem. I don't hear gunfire, and there are much fewer houses being burned down. My guess is that the gangs have worn themselves out, drunk all the liquor, and sort of died off. I found two guys dead one morning up towards Temples, and they had been sick. Like Tom, the guy Dad had said was bombed out of his skull. Which means drunk.

Kim started to drink everything in sight when she came here, so I poured the stuff out the bar sink, and that stopped that. Then she wanted to go house crashing to get some more, and I said definitely no. We are safe here, no one has ever come in here, and not to hunt for trouble. She cried some, and that was that.

Right after she came, almost the next day, the water got up over what used to be our back lawn, and came near the patio. Then the rain stopped, and after a few days the water went down. That next summer, I set fire to the brush down at the tunnel, and what little rain we had the next year washed the rest of the junk on through the tunnel. And no one is throwing their garden cuttings in the wash anymore, so it still works.

I could do a lot more around her, but the water is down to a dribble, and it is better for us to wash ourselves and clothes in the creek, and save what little water comes in for the dishes. Kim thinks we are very fancy here because we eat at a table on painted dishes. When she was little and her mother was there, they ate on plastic out of the microwave and threw it away. I guess that was efficient, but Mom didn't have plastic plates, so we have to make do with what we have. Gas is the only thing we still have, and I don't see how after all the fires downtown Santa Barbara, and the earthquake last year it still works. But it does. Even so, I've been cutting wood with a cross-buck saw, and stacking it in the garage, in case we have to start using the BBQ. There's quite a lot of charcoal for it too, about twenty pounds, and now that I see it may be useful, I have rousted more from houses around us.

What I don't have is time to read as much as I would like. Non-fiction about the way the world used to be is very interesting, but it makes me feel useless that it was all, or I guess at least the United States part of it, destroyed in the riots and the crazy times that followed. I have no way of really knowing, but if there is anything left of the old life, it sure never comes near this part of Santa Barbara and Montecito. And, after what I've seen in just this neighborhood, I guess I don't want to go out and find out.

I like to read fiction, but not twentieth century fiction. Travel books and Mom's Art History books give me a pretty good picture of Europe and the US before my parents were born. So that's interesting to read novels about; I can see the places, and imagine it. I was too young to have seen much of pre-riot life, and stories about just before that just don't make as much sense to me as the others.

Kim is like Yin and Yang. She wants me to tell her things will be all right, and after we make love, she always cries. I spend a lot of time making her feel better, the way I used to with the dogs, to the point that she runs our life, and I do the work.

I tried to teach her to read, but she's not interested. I tried to teach her chess from a book I borrowed at Dr. Wilkensons, up the street. No go. She watches me work, asks me is everything is OK, and we make love. The Doc had books about that too, and they're pretty helpful. Kim doesn't seem to care much how we do it, but I think experimentation is rewarding.

Which brings me to the point. First couple of times we made love, I just did it. Like a kid with no brains. Then I remembered that screwing is making babies too. That I don't want. Not until things get straightened out, anyhow. So I scouted the houses in the block for information and Trojans. There are other brands too, but what with the looting and vandalism, not much in people's bathrooms is useful. The doctors house had some books about birth control, and another place, where someone's gardener lived, had a lot of foil packages of large sized ribbed condoms, which seemed OK. But we got through what I had pretty fast, and I tried to teach Kim the Rhythm Method from the book, but that was too hard for her, so I had to plan that too.

Except that I didn't plan very well. Last month Kim started being sick at her stomach. I did what I could, and hoped it was green bananas or something. In one of Docs books, I diagnosed Kim as pregnant. Good God!

Years ago, when Mom and Dad first left, I found the Book of Common Prayer. I used to read out of it, sometimes things I remembered from All Saints by the Sea, and sometimes new things. It sounded so smooth, and I always felt better when I read out loud. Yin and Yang liked it, because they always came and sat with me when I read out.

After Kimmie came, I didn't read much, but the other day, about sun down, I got it out again, and read some to Kim. It put her to sleep, and sounded great to me. Better when read out loud, like Longfellow, who is not much unless you do him out loud.

So, the day after I buried old Yang, I slipped down the wash as soon as the sun gave enough light, kept in the shadows behind the burned-out wrecks of the Miramar cottages, and up Eucalyptus Lane to the church. Burned, of course, but I slid in among the fallen beams, up where the alter was. I kneeled down for a while, and said some things I remembered, and I asked for God to take this baby before I have to take care of it. I can't. It's too scary, and I am too alone, what with Kim running the place. I couldn't keep her safe, and a baby too. I don't even know how to help at the birth. The pictures scare the Hell out of me.

God didn't say whether he heard me or not, and I guess that was an answer in itself.

I don't go down this way very often, because, despite my incendiary efforts, the tunnel is kind of choked up, and sometimes I think someone is hidden in the brush. Anyway, this morning, I looked in a house beyond the tunnel, on Fernald Point Road. They had a statue, a little white thing, of a baby, so maybe God did send me a message. I stuffed the thing in the side pocket of Dad's hunting jacket, which I usually wore these mornings because it has lots of pockets. The house that had the baby had some dead bodies in it, gang personnel, I should think, but they were old enough not to stink. I borrowed some canned stuff, and, for about the fortieth time, canned nuts from the bar. Don't these drunks know enough to take them?

So, what with one thing and another, I'm home, and I'm going to have to raise a baby. The only sounds are coyotes, who go back and forth to the beach like it was the old Freeway. They scare me, and it puts me in about the mood Kimmie is in. She spends most days in Mom's closet. Mom will be annoyed when she returns and finds all her stuff on the floor, but what can I do. It helps Kimmie.

Sun going down in pink light. I can hear the surf, because the wind is coming from that way. I can't use the BBQ or the wood, because the smoke might lead someone here. The gas is too thin to stay lighted, so I guess were at the end of that resource. And I am absolutely alone in the world, held here by Kimmie and the baby. I don't know whether to beat my head on the wall, to cry, or to swallow hard and say the Scout oath and keep going.

Is this all there is to life? The books don't say so, but is all that over? All over the world?

Over.

Deadly History

1

NEW YORK, the First Day

I took a bribe knowing what it was, but not exactly knowing why.

Frances moved papers on her glass and chromium desk, and asked why not?

'Why not which? Take it? or know why it was offered?' Edward Hamilton, PhD, expected clear questions from this lawyer, beautiful or not.

'Well, either, I guess.' She said 'eye-ther' in a mocking way, and smiled encouragingly. New York birds blew past outside the tight-sealed windows, unconcerned with the interview within.

'I guess it began when his cottage blew up. My boss' cottage. He was killed, and things have been goofy ever since. And now, I'm called to New York for who-knows what reason. I need to know whether I've been wrong.'

'Would you mind to begin from the beginning? If I can help, I need to know the whole story.'

He took a breath, and began. 'My ex-father-in-law got to be the head of the Foundation. So he was in charge of the Foundation's grants and scholarships. Fellowships, actually. Maybe it was a conflict of interest for him, but he gave me a grant. Maybe because it got me out of Santa Barbara, which I guess he wanted. But it also let me write the book I'd proposed.' Edward watched Frances Russell's beautiful hands. Strong but sensitive, Edward thought with no basis whatsoever for such an observation.

'He sent you to Ireland?' Frances prompted.

Edward explained that the book in progress was called 'The Effects of Popular Beliefs and Common Experiences Upon a People.' About Ireland. He tried to enlarge upon his topic; it sounded unreal in this steel and neutral law office, this tiny room among the hundreds of gray-toned offices within the huge law firm his buddy at Yale had recommended. Hundreds of yards of gray carpet which matched the gray of the sky, and harmonized with the other tall buildings. The whole thing seemed to float, disconnected from the real world.

'And now, there's the demand from Julia Armbruster Vickery that I come to New York to see her. What's funny, is that the ticket is paid on her credit card!'

Frances said he'd have to explain who Julia was, and what the source of her ticket had to do with the Foundation.

'She's the Chairman of the Trustees, and her mother, Leila Armbruster, the pancake queen, started the Foundation. If the business she has with me is the Foundation's, why not have them issue the ticket? And what's she so cross about?'

'Cross?'

'Yup. Barked into the telephone, 'No more evasions Dr Hamilton,' she said, 'Be here immediately.' Which is why I want to know, going into the interview, if there's anything wrong with my Fellowship contract. I can refund what's been paid so far, and I won't give them any trouble if I was in the wrong.'

'Evasions? That sounds odd, as you had never talked to her before.' Frances said.

'Not never met her. It's just that I've hardly even spoken to the woman. Introduced, said pleased, and that's about it.'

Frances brought him back to the question for which he was paying a consulting fee. 'And what makes you think that your grant, your Fellowship, is a bribe?'

His eyes focussed beyond the view, as he framed his answer. Clear, roundish: believer's eyes. Longish brown lashes: a lover's eyes. 'I was a Resident Scholar at the Foundation for Historical Research. Santa Barbara, California is where it is. When I had been there a few months, I married the daughter of a Fellow. Then the Director was killed in an explosion on campus, and my father-in-law became the Director.' He was distracted by the images of Pinky-the-lush, poor Dr T, and Bernard in the air outside Frances's office. Slide shows of Santa Barbara flickered past like the birds.

Frances waited, then said, 'Lawyers find that silence tends to rush a client into needful explanations. But it really is time for you to tell me about it.'

'Sorry. I had a PhD from Princeton, and then two of my history books were published. I was invited to live at the Foundation, actually in Montecito, and write another book. The Armbruster Foundation has its campus on the estate of the family that, started the Foundation. Well, I had been on campus about six months. One of the Fellows had the most knockout daughter! We fell for each other, were married on the campus, and given a cottage on the grounds. That was before my ex-father-in-law became the Director.'

Frances asked, 'Ex-father-in-law, meaning no longer married?

Edward Hamilton picked up his story: Living with Pinky had been Hell. Just as she had easily fallen into his arms, she fell into the arms of all who welcomed her, and volunteered to many who had not asked, but were nevertheless willing. And drink? The Foundation staff and Fellows took dinner together twice a week, and an open bar was available on those nights. Pinky only began her drinking in the living room. After dinner, she left campus, returning, or being returned in various conditions late, or early the next morning.

He had grabbed a spectacular body, and never looked beyond her pouting face. Somehow marriage had freed her from any sense of restraint. She accepted his ring and embarked on a round of insults for which Edward blamed himself as much as she did. Not that he knew what he'd done to trigger her actions, and he said as much to Pinky's father.

'S.Bernard Esbenshade, PhD, LLD was sort of the administrative cappo of the Foundation. Not really an historian, but an academic who thrived on keeping order and knew where all the pencils and typewriter ribbons were. Bernard told me, "Pinky, as you call her, is not unlike her mother, I'm afraid. Believe me," the old boy said, "it's nothing you have done, nor anything you have failed to do." Well, after that, all I had to deal with was embarrassment. After three months, Pinky was again living in the main house in a little room next to her father's. The institution closed around the story of the failed marriage, treating both parties as innocent and without fault. That probably sounds odd to you.'

Francis shook her head so that her light hair moved gently. 'I'm sorry.'

After about a year on campus, the Executive Director, Dr John Tscherbateff, called me into his, office. It's a spooky place. It was the Armbruster's library, all dark wood, and facing North into dense shade. I always thought Dr T grew lichen I there. Anyway, he started formally. 'Dr Hamilton, you are the coming light of this place.' He went on to tell me that my third book, that I had just turned over to the Institutes publishing department was pretty good, in his opinion. They were going to issue it simultaneously with a commercial publisher. And doing it immediately. He actually smiled and tried to thump me on the back.

"Have I seen your last book?"

'Maybe. It's been out some time now, and I guess commercial sales are pretty good. PBS asked about doing a docu-drama, but I don't want it fictionalized or monkeyed with. Anyway, Dr T was not only the head of the Foundation, he was the widower of the woman who had donated the money to start the Foundation. A man of enormous professional and financial clout. The compliment kind of overwhelmed me. Astonished me, in fact. That day, Dr T had more to say, "I would like to name you as a Fellow as soon as you can suggest a line of research or a topic. You would, I assume, accept a Fellowship?" Would? Damn right. Sixty thousand a year, all expenses covered, unlimited staff assistance, and guaranteed publication. Dr T believed that, once a topic was selected, the historian Fellows were to proceed right to completion; if commercial publishers declined the book, or the Fellow's own University presses declined it, the Foundation would bring out the book, regardless of the lack of market. A scholars dream.'

Edward's long face recalled the pride he had felt then, then his face changed. 'Not long after that, Dr T was killed in an explosion.'

'Sorry. Before you go on to the poor man's accident, could you tell me how the Executive Director felt about the break-up of your marriage?'

'Tscherbateff said, "My own feeling is that Maud, as you say Pinky, must solve her problems for herself and do so off campus. I intend to make certain that her father agrees with me!" That surprised me, because Pinky had been rather a favorite at the Foundation. A much loved terrible child; or had been until her drinking and sleeping around had become a scandal. Bernard, her father, was the dog of all work for Dr T; whatever was drudgery or boring, Bernard Esbenshade did it. He is dull, loyal and yet the rock of the organization.'

Francis pushed the water carafe at her new client, but he went on without noticing.

'I just couldn't imagine that Dr T had put himself out so much just for me. In fact, I dismissed it as just a change that happened to come at the same time as his Fellowship was offered. Much later I learned that Dr T had issued an ultimatum to Pinky's father, along the lines that "Either she goes, or you both go." That was an unequivocal instruction to a man I thought that he needed!'

'The night of my talk with Dr T, I heard Pinky, drunk and loud, arguing with some man who'd joined her at the pool. The estate's swimming pool is in a Moorish kind of garden, almost entirely screened from the cottages on the grounds. Given the nature of water, some sounds travel to the nearest cottages. In the warm evening, Pinky's voice came loud and clear. "The Hell with old Johnny! I'm not going any frigging where! And he can't make me! So you just come on." She said less, less audibly, and then there was more noise, an altercation in fact. Then silence. I didn't like the sound of any of that, so I got out of bed, dressed, and was in the pool garden few minutes later. The place was empty. Some beer cans stood on the patio table, and the pads of two chaises were on the deck, probably ready for...Ready. I was disgusted, and started back to my own cottage.

'I hoped that Dr T, whose cottage was on the opposite side of the pool, but out of sight in the dark, had not heard Pinky. I hit the sack again. Much later, unable to sleep, I heard a door close, and I got up again. This time, I walked through the pool garden and up the east walk towards the mansion. Three cottages of the age and style of the main house stand along the east walk. Everything was pale that night. Full moon, I guess.

'Up ahead, I saw Esbenshade walking up the path to the main house, just beyond Dr T's cottage. I asked him if everything was OK. He said, "Yes, Pinky's fine," he kind of waved, and went on towards the house where his suite is, and where Pinky lived. Relieved, I went back to bed. Then, when I was hardly asleep, BANG! Sounded like the universe had imploded!'

Frances asked if the explosion was a bomb.

'Dr T's cottage was blown to pieces! It was an old building, the same age as the mansion itself. Apparently the gas pipes corroded, and gas leaked into the walls of the building, was ignited by the water heater's pilot light, and poor Dr T was killed.'

'But you got your Fellowship anyway, apparently.'

'That's what's screwy. Somewhere during the funeral week, one of the older Fellows told me that Dr T had ordered Pinky to leave the Foundation grounds. Forbidden her to stay. I figured my time there was over because Bernard seemed likely to succeed Dr T as Executive Director. And he hovered over Pinky, trying to protect her. I figured I'd become persona non grata, and was expecting to leave.'

'Bernard called me into his office, still the small one in those weeks when the name of Dr Ts successor was unknown. I figured to be severed from my resident scholarship. Instead, Bernard said, 'You, my son, are to be my first appointment as Fellow of the Foundation. I have Dr Ts notes on your project, and I'm very much in favor of it. I just regret that we can't tell anyone about it until the Trustees announce my own promotion. So mum's the word until then!'

'I remember Bernard moved some papers on his desk. He has a huge scarab ring, Egyptian, old, dark with a funny light inside it. Nasty thing, somehow. No matter, I was so weak. I just stood there and said 'Thank you.'

'Well, the Trustees knew you were married to Pinky, and surely Dr. Esbenshade discussed your appointment with them. So far, it sounds like you got the Fellowship on your own merit.'

'There's more. He not only confirmed the promotion, but also said I should plan to write the whole thing in Ireland. He said that when I'd finished, I'd come back, and the marriage for which he had hoped so much would be over and forgotten. In other words, I scram, Pinky gets a divorce, and we all forget the whole thing.'

'Why in Ireland.'

'I have used her jumbled history to illustrate my argument. Which is that perceptions make a country what it is as much as the events themselves.'

'I see,' Frances made minor adjustments to her desk pad. 'After you left, was there any arrangement for supervising your work?'

'Sure. Every scholar is required to submit weekly reports to the Executive Director. If we're actually writing, we usually send that week's pages. I use e-mail. During research periods, we summarize the data, and indicate how it fits in the context of our work; I make those reports too.'

Frances said all that sounded perfectly straightforward.

'What's your concern? Ed? Eddie? Ned? Do you mind?' She made it sound friendly.

'Eddie, I guess. I've been Edward all my life, so OK, Eddie to you.' Great ankles, he held his breath for a second as she crossed to the side table, poured water for both of them, and took them from sight behind the desk. The ankles, that is.

'Well, I've never been satisfied that the Fellowship was entirely on merit. I think Dr T meant well, and did propose a Fellowship, but sending a new Fellow off to the ends of civilization? That's radical. And done, I'm afraid, so Bernard can keep Pinky with him! They're very close, her mother being long gone.'

'Gone? Deceased?'

'No, run off with the local tennis pro, who inherited a bundle about then. Pinky's mother is on her third millionaire, but nowhere near Santa Barbara; I've never even seen her, let alone talked to the mother.'

Frances asked Eddie to get on with his suspicions.

He said that was it.

She said the elements of a contract were intent of the parties, performance of something of value, payment, and time. But, the document had to be read to be sure that he'd done his part. Frances wound up her thoughts, saying, 'All right, I see your worry. Largely a moral issue, but let me read the contract you brought, and I'll call you tomorrow.'

In the actual event, 'tomorrow' proved to be a date for drinks that same day, an hour or so after Frances' law office closed.

The King Cole Bar at the St Regis, below the Maxfield Parish mural, wherein cartoonish characters quaff before a sublime painting of California at sunset; a picture with a wasted foreground. Oddly, the luminous mountains and reflective foliage in the painting are those of Santa Barbara and Montecito.

On a banquette in that dim and elegant drinking room. Ale for him, and scotch rocks for her. Two brunettes, one set of green eyes, one set of blue. An attractive couple. Where the woman had the lovely profile of a cameo, the man was distinctly beaky.

Where she smiled easily, he was serious, quiet in speech. Where he was rumpled looking, even for the nineteen nineties, she was crisply professional; corduroys and tweed versus Donna Karan.

'You haven't told me all there is to tell. Let's hear the rest.'

Eddie shifted uncomfortably. 'It's stupid. Someone broke into my house in Ireland. Nothing taken that I can identify. But a computer disc, with an article for the Irish Times was copied. And notes about that were moved.'

'What was in the article?'

'Just a brief answer to a journalist's question as to why I was in Ireland. A question prompted by a nice helpful librarian in Dublin.' A librarian of the milkiest complexion and silkiest red hair; an irresistibly girl. 'The article briefed the topic of my book, and described the Foundation. And I threw in a tribute to Dr T.'

'Esbenshade saw the article?'

'I e-mailed it, just normally, and I'm sure he did.'

'We'd better look at it again, because something in that article raised a question in someone's mind. From what you say, in Bernard's mind. Can you get a copy? Oh, and was it published?'

'Sure. That's why fooling with the disc was so stupid! Everything on it was in the Times story.'

Frances said she would have thought one might have several versions of the article on the disc or notes of parts later cut from the article. She did not move away as his knee grazed her thigh, as if accidentally.

'No. You see a professional writer, and most historians are that, knows he's to write five-hundred words, a thousand words or whatever, and plans that many, and writes almost to the word or page the count required. Second nature.' His knees came at last to rest against Frances' warm thigh, having brushed by once and found them unlikely to move away.

Eddie was bold because he'd finally decided to do something out of character. The decision emboldened him in several ways. Historians are passive, and he'd decided not to be. He had to know if he'd earned the luxuries of time and comfort of last year on merit or as pay for being out of the way. And he had to know why he was being summoned and investigated.

'There's one other thing. Travelers from the Foundation pass through Wexford as if it were London; it's not on the way anywhere! Yet Fred Mancuso came through on his way to Budapest! And Dr Franklin visited on his way to Rome. Nothing accidental about that.'

Frances thought it normal enough to check on employees or sub-contractors working away from the home base. 'But what you describe does seem bizarre. How often?'

He thought they'd been coming about every six weeks. 'Usually overnight, and friendly, but asking lots of questions too. About his work, his view of the world in general. Very talkative. Like I'm being interviewed, or something.'

Frances agreed that the frequency and close interest was odd, but might reflect Dr Esbenshade's concern that he had done something 'different' in creating the absent professor routine for Eddie. 'Just describe Dr Esbenshade for me, so I get the picture better.'

He took a breath, 'J Bernard Esbenshade: Thrifty build, as though his parents intended to waste nothing in conceiving him. They gave him no extra bone, no extra flesh, and no smile! Bred to go straight to his objective. In the Renaissance he would have been Pope.'

A little electricity passed between them. Nice tingling.

They discussed the break-in, the Foundation's operations, and forked into personal questions. After a second drink was ordered, Edward said something about knowing he didn't look much like a historian.

Frances giggled, 'Rumpled corduroys and a tweed jacket look exactly like a historian. How did you come to be one?

'When I was the age for HotWheels I had all the models, spent all my time playing with them, or dreaming about the layouts I'd make if only I had more track. Then I read Gibbon.'

'Decline and Fall of the Roman Empire,' Frances interposed, mildly showing off.

'Right. No one today would want to write as he did, but I fell for the periodic sentence anyway. All that big rolling paragraphic structure, wrapped around the lives of Emperors, the fate of nations! Well, I'm still stuck. How things happen, and what the world is all about!'

Frances asked if that was what the current book would be about. She sat perfectly still, apparently unwilling to change the pressure of his leg against hers.

'I'm trying to explain a way to write comprehensive history. To get away from economic history, or great man theories, or grandeur and decline concepts. I think peoples and nations develop from their collective experiences. Those interact with neighboring cultures, until merged and shared. Common experiences dictate the responses of society at any time. For example, the invasions of Ireland in the twelve hundreds by King John set the Irish against the English. And even though the ethnic and tribal experience of the Irish is far far different now than it was eight hundred years ago, the responses are still conditioned by those events. Needless to admit that the English have reinforced their impact on the Irish frequently since that time. I'm showing how the two cultures could have lived more beneficially had the mind set been different on any subsequent occasion.' Their closeness on the banquette was beginning to be in some way preparatory.

'Sounds almost impossibly broad...'

Eddie admitted problems of scholarship and reason. And he bragged a little that he was up to it all.

2

NEW YORK, The Second Day

Frances tried to summarize. 'I believe you are performing a service, living up to your contract. They intended that you write a certain book, and you are doing so. You send regular reports of your progress, regular expenses in compliance with the Foundation's policies. The only thing I haven't heard is that someone in Santa Barbara acknowledges your reports.'

Eddie moved against Frances. 'You bet. Bernard is something of a pest. Debates what I send in long paragraphs, then agrees with my treatment, or mostly does. Thank God he doesn't pick on my writing the way he does with everyone else.'

'But he shows he's read it, right?'

'Right. He drives some of the Fellows nuts, because he picks on grammar and syntax. Nit picks. But he's slacked off on my English lessons; maybe he doesn't care much what I do, tethered out on the moors!'

'You think that Bernard wasn't interested in your book?'

His gripe amounted to the observation that Bernard appeared to accept Eddy's writing as he sent it. 'Guess I'm unique in that respect. He has no reason to like me; thought

Pinky walked on water, and I know he thought I should have been able to manage her better. No way!'

Frances repeated her opinion that he was engaged to do serious work, and all he had to do to feel comfortable with his contract was to complete the book. Then, to turn their interests into a more personal vein, she asked what historians, he himself, liked to read.

He explained about Prescott of 'Peru' and 'Schevill,' Frederick Schaevill, Violet Wedgewood, and someone called David Hackett Fischer, who wrote the best book I know of about history. 'Historians Fallacies'.*

Frances laughed in her throaty, and tried again to get un-historical. 'You do have spare time?'

'Sure. I ride. Horses. I've ridden everything from a dam above Aswan to the Arabians in Scotland, as Rudolph Rassendyl almost said.'

Whooping, Frances caused heads to turn, 'What!'

'Anthony Hope, 'Prisoner of Zenda'. Opening line. Only he said he'd shot everything from the rapids above Aswan to the grouse on the moors of Scotland. Arabs for moors.'

Frances knew old movies. 'Ronald Coleman as both Rudolf Rassendyl and Ruppert of Zenda. But that's fiction, not history!'

Eddie said he was allowed to read anything printed, so why not fiction? And what did she do in her spare time, anyway?

She swept her hair away from her face, saying, 'I'm starved. Let's order something. And I ride (even side saddle), jump horses and, horrors, hunt foxes!'

* *Harper & Row's Torchbook Series*

No wonder she had such a responsive thigh; takes a horsewoman, he concluded. And eye lids which tilted up, asking questions, forbidding nothing.

In mid-evening, Edward realized that his adventure started here, and started now.

Frances responded to his next advance, saying, when their Gotham sandwiches were finished, 'Coffee at my place? But look. This is the nineties.'

'...which means we have only ourselves to please.'

'Which means, we proceed with caution. Sorry. We have a future, but it's going to open a little more...'

'Could it be passionate caution?' Edward asked innocently, his hand covering hers.

On East Sixty Second, in an apartment as luxurious as it's three tiny rooms would allow, all pale colors which flattered a brown-haired woman, Frances stood in the bed room door, well wrapped in a robe the color of pale apricots. 'Let me make this easy,' Frances cinched up the belt of her robe in a cautionary way.

Edward was trying to shake the condoms out of the package he had bought at a drugstore detour on the way to Frances' flat. He looked up, embarrassed.

She continued, 'I'll say it; no, I have not gone to bed with anyone who was not wearing a condom during the term of development of any known sexually transmitted disease or infection.'

Edward laughed, they both laughed, and fell in a tangle upon each other.

'Nor I...' At the appropriate time, with laughter as each tried to unpack the wretched condom, the device was used. And, later, another.

In the morning, Frances told her office she would be in late.

Fred, her secretary, remembered the tall client who'd come from Ireland, and thought his own thoughts. Not that his boss was available to anyone Fred knew about, but rather that she'd spent so much time getting her coat on, checking her face and hair before she left to meet this Dr Hamilton for drinks. Good for her, he thought.

Up on East Sixty Second Street, a breakfast conference was under way.

'Let's prepare for your meeting. We can start with the fact that your contract and Fellowship are absolutely in order. What else could have disturbed Mrs Vickery? Would you run through it again?'

'OK, thanks. Then what…? Mrs Vickery barked at me like a sergeant! That's part of why I came to your law firm, and I guess I have wasted your time on the dumb bribe idea.' Eddie's eyes crinkled, his way of smiling.

'Best to be sure; no fault. How else would we have met?'

They smiled at each other, but Eddie's relaxed face was less smile, and more expression.

Frances insisted. 'You're off campus, and not under Bernard's daily influence. It strikes me that if she wants straight impressions of Bernard as Executive Director, you might seem a very good source. In fact you might be antagonistic, and not just because you're an ex-son-in-law.'

Eddie denied anything except respect for Bernard, but the denial was more for form than otherwise. Eddie thought it wrong to bad-mouth anyone absent from the discussion, unless they were historical figures of course.

'Well, I think Julia Vickery thinks there's something going on in California, and wants more information. Did you ever think that something's going on there that the Trustees are too thick to spot?'

Frances poured more coffee, somehow contriving to soothe the duck's feathers on the back of Eddie's head as she did it. Then she asked him to tell her all about Ireland. What he did there, and how he lived.

'It's a good house for a scholar. Regency. Meant for someone of refinement when built in 1815 or 1820. 'Maybe a retired military officer, a veteran of the Napoleonic wars. But built with knowledge of Greek and Roman details. It lies in a fold of the hills, at the top of a south-facing valley. At the foot of the valley, a few houses make a village, and beyond, Bantry Bay. The south coast of Ireland. A funnel of green leading to a beautiful blue piece of the Atlantic.

'And my neighbor has a dozen horses, and we ride and sometimes hunt! Ideal!' He worked every day, and wearied Frances detailing the way a historian works.

As, she thought, a lawyer preparing a case would proceed. The difference being that the lawyer strives to build arguments favoring the client, while the historian, or at least Edward, insisted upon marshalling facts, memories and other's opinions in an effort to understand and explain what went on at some point in the past. Frances asked, 'And you are alone all this time?'

He said 'Mostly,' not caring to tell about the pretty girls he squired around Dublin every few weeks. And especially not wanting to tell this attractive brunette that he'd learned a little more about love-making from the Dublin girls than he had from Pinky. Indeed, Pinky Esbenshade had always complained that he was a lousy lover. The evidence of his experiences in Dublin suggested otherwise to him.

The exchange satisfied Frances that this giant historian was neither living with or actively married. She had been interested to hear herself ask the question "Alone?" as until then she had thought that her attraction to Eddie was purely physical. Interesting.

Following the train of her own thoughts, Francis said, 'You are still as single-minded as the little boy who collected HotWheels. I'll bet you work until your muscles twitch, then ride your neighbor's horses until they are tired, and then come home to work some more.'

'About right.' He did not add that sex was simply an occasional need, loneliness not an issue. 'I have neighbors. The Tolynals of Tollynoll House. Spelled differently, because the ownership skipped a couple of generations of the same family. They lost their house, and had to have it back the first time any of them get the money. Where else does history hangs over the present; it's everywhere you look! This guy is something in the government, vague about it. We ride together, and I pay the board on a couple of his horses. It was Tolynal who saw the spy, raking my house with field glasses.'

'Fiction again?' Frances laughed.

'No, History. It must have been the guy who snooped, who read the Irish Times disc.'

'And you're sure there was nothing on that disc to worry anyone?'

'Nothing! Only thing I said worth remembering is a neat phrase about Dr Tscherbateff: The man historians needed to bring them into modern times.'

He looked at his watch. ' Nearly ten! Time to go and see the Chairman,' he said shifting dishes, as tidy people do.

Frances tended to correct things as she went: 'No, you'll see the Chair or Chairperson: chairman is derogatory.'

'It is not! Moreover a chair is inanimate, and can't preside. The job is chairman; it's like the Postmaster, it's the name of the job, and...'

Frances laughed in her happy way, and said, 'Oh get on with it! You're hopeless!'

Confident, cool, strutting a little like a well satisfied rooster, Eddie strolled up to Fifth Avenue to Sixty Eighth Street, and turned into a lobby so refined it seemed undecorated. Empty but for the butlerish person who admitted him. He was handed over to a liveried man who drove the elevator up several floor, and pushed him out in an ample lobby whose main function seemed to be to house Mrs Vickery's front door. It opened, and there she was.

Julia Armbruster Vickery was tall. Steel gray hair, lashed back with a silk scarf. Chic no doubt, but a law unto herself. Individualistic. Who else would wear ten rows of graduated pearls early in the morning?

Julia Armbruster Vickery, author of historic novels, a professor of English at Columbia University, sometime hostess of a syndicated talk show on Public Television. Married to some Wall Street guru. Tall as Eddie himself. He saw it would be impossible to whisper sweet nothings into her ear, as most guys couldn't reach it.

Slim, elegant. She shook hands briskly, and let him follow her into a squarish room hanging just above Central Park's trees; her private garden, it seemed. Fine period pieces, expensive contemporary sculpture, comfortable colors, everything simple and clearly the very best.

At the attack, she asked, 'Why didn't you answer my inquiry?'

Trying not to be defensive, 'Sorry. What inquiry?'

She spoke firmly, and directly to the point that she had asked the Foundation to have Edward telephone her. He had not, so she had written to him, care of the Foundation, and no reply had come. Not the courtesy she expected! Demanded!

Edward patiently explained that he had never had either communication. And would most certainly have returned the Chairman's call.

Julia stared at him as if she could see the truth in his face. 'Bernard! I'd like to wring his neck sometimes. Pompous.' Then she said, still demanding, 'I want you to write my stepfather's biography. Is it yes?'

Julia had not suggested he sit down, and they stood half a room apart. Altogether an uncomfortable situation. Edward bowed slightly, thinking the setting called for a little decorum, 'Sorry. I admired Dr Tscherbateff, but he hardly knew me...Why me?'

'Your letter of condolence, your other writings. You write well, better than historians do. And I think you liked my stepfather. I can tell that you appreciate what he intended to do.'

'I'm flattered. More than I can say, because I admired Dr T, very much. Thank you.'

'Then why not answer 'yes'?'

Edward hesitated. It was the right move, because Julia indicated a chair, and sat close to him, almost in a friendly way.

'That cuts right to the heart of my concerns. Let's have some coffee. It helps me to think, and I want to be very careful about this. Or would you rather have a drink...'

In the event, a servant brought coffee on a wheeled cart which seemed to have been sent up by the Metropolitan Museum especially to carry the treasures of cups, pot and cake dish standing on it.

Pouring, Julia seemed to shift her thoughts slightly. 'I hope your book will have some little influence on putting the Foundation back on course.'

Cautiously he asked, 'How is it off course? I've been working away from Santa Barbara all year.' Then he saw her expression: amused, a little patronizing. He went on, 'Well, I guess I know part of what you mean. My former father-in-law is more nearly the schoolteacher, the conventional historian, secretive and non-collegial. But he is rather grand, you must admit.'

'Pompous, more aptly,' Julia said, still not wholly pleased with Edward. 'Have you actually read the last few publications? And you still defend Bernard?'

Edward considered that briefly, and tried to lead Julia in another direction, 'Maybe on the edge of pompous, but then dignity isn't such a bad thing.'

Julia was only briefly distracted. 'My step-father had dignity, but did you ever see him deliberately embarrass anyone, or put himself first if there was anyone else who might possibly be pleased to be first? Now don't be loyal! Be objective, as Dr T would have been.'

Edward finally said what had been on his mind for several years. Bernard had edited the individuality out of every book brought out under the Foundation's logo. Reduced good, and sometimes witty prose to group-speak. Edited unpopular insights from books, reducing them to card catalogues. Prevented original research in topics regarded by the literary establishment as untouchable. Imposed all the sins of censorship on the Fellows.

'Exactly,' said Julia, dropping her large hand on to her knee. 'You have it in one. Go on...'

Reluctantly, Edward added that Bernard held court at Villa del Torre with such stiff punctilio that he induced fear and awe in outsiders, and paralyzed the Fellows. 'Miss dinner on the stated dining-in nights, and you're frozen out of general conversation for weeks! Damn nuisance!'

'You are aware that none of this accords with my stepfather's intentions?'

'Not exactly, but Dr Ts style was pretty relaxed. The grand setting and elaborate meals were, for him, I think, just a means of prolonging an informal exchange of views. A free-for-all of civilized intellects.'

'And the publications?' Julia poured more coffee.

'Dr T expected fresh inquiries, original research, and I know he admired fine writing. He read some draft of mine, and said, 'Write as you speak, but with more polish!' I've tried that ever since.'

Julia commented that he wrote better than he spoke, but perhaps he didn't like her inquisition.

'No, I don't mind. But you are the Chairman of the Board of Trustees. Why ask me things about which you have already formed conclusions?'

'I'm only one vote, but I'm not happy. I want the founder's views restated, not the institution demolished. That's why I want you to undertake the biography.' Edward rose, walked to the bookcase holding the Foundation's publications. Turning back to Julia, he said 'Not resisting, but trying for a practical answer: how can I stop the work I'm doing to do this for you? I've another year's work on my own book, and my grant ends then.'

'Bernard has plenty of money to work with; ask him to reform your grant. He has total discretion, unlimited authority, you know. And that may be his mistake…'

'Mistake?' Edward hadn't thought in terms of mistakes.

'He takes no advice. Is sufficient unto himself. That's what's the matter. Had the Trustees not formed the habit, under my Mother's chairmanship, of not questioning the Executive Director, I think Bernard might have been a capable administrator.'

Julia had substantially relaxed, concluding that Edward was the man she had, from reading his books, expected. 'Do we call you Edward, or is there a diminutive? You may call me Julia. We are going to be good friends before all this is over, so I say, let us begin now.'

That made Edward shy. Nicknames always had. Pinky had called him Ned and Neddie-boy! Some almost forgotten girl had called him Ed, and a silly Dublin girl said 'Hampty'. Eddie as Frances said it was OK, but he wanted that to be between them. Trying not to sound too formal, he softened his face, and said, 'I'm just plain Edward. That's it! No tricks in that.'

Julia accepted that, and Eddie continued. And, just by asking, you think I can get my grant reformed?

'Probably the reason he hasn't put me in touch with you is that a biography is precisely what he doesn't want! We'll never know until you ask? Will we? And I will, on the next occasion, ask a rude question at the Board meeting...No, nothing to embarrass you! But he will understand my question!'

Edward shook his head, saying he would try, and was headed, in any case, to Santa Barbara.

'May I ask why? Not curiosity, but a real need to know.'

'Well, as just said, Bernard has edited the brains out of all the new publications. It's all gooey stuff with the author's point of view excised. But I send my week's work in, get comments back which are so detached that I'm feeling like I'm falling without a net! And not one word about style. His penchant is correcting style! I want to know why?'

'Well now! Bernard and I are of the same mind, this one time! Your writing stands alone. It's fine!'

'Thanks. But, I have some other whys too.'

'Go on.'

Edward told her about the break in, but excised mention of what had been disturbed, saying instead, 'Foundation papers had been disarranged, but nothing else; speaks of a selective bit of snooping. And I want to know why.'

'Please, Edward, let me know what you conclude, and please, write the biography.'

In the vestibule, shaking hands good-bye, Edward said, 'Bernard runs a one man show, so even if I do take on the Dr T book, I'm not very confident it will be within my grant. Something to do when I get a teaching position, next year or so.'

Julia said that wouldn't do. The biography had to be written this year, because, 'I do not want to wind up the Foundation, but I've made up my mind.'

'Wind it up? You could do that? End the Foundation?'

Julia stood against her marble door jamb, defiantly, proudly, 'If we could show that it was being used for advancement of any person, canon of beliefs or mismanaged, all the money falls back in Jack's and my hands. Scandal, misrepresentations, anything unsavory. After we pay around two hundred million to the IRS for estate taxes, that is. If I didn't have far more than I need for myself, I might just do that.'

'Jack?'

Julia smiled, 'Jack Tscherbateff, Dr T's son by a former marriage. My step-brother.'

'How does he get any of the money if the Foundation is wound up.'

'My Mother provided he gets twenty-five percent of the wind-up proceeds, say around seventy million.'

Edward showed his surprise. 'Wow! Wonder he isn't pressing you to work on a wind-up.'

Julia said that was not Jack's sphere of interest. 'He won't even come on the Board of Trustees. Stuffy, he says, and quite correctly.'

Edward felt stiff and stupid, standing at the open door like a guest who doesn't know how to say good bye. 'Very well, I will propose to Bernard that he extend my fellowship, and write the new book. But, you have another agenda, don't you?'

'Just bear in mind what I've said. I'd be grateful for anything that would exert a little leverage on dear Bernard. Now go, and for God's sake, take care of yourself!'

That evening at Frances' apartment, Eddie said 'Reliable scandal, I guess she meant.'

'Including peculation or, Aha! Pederasty among the pedagogues! Miscegenation between the cleaning ladies and the Fellows. All grist…'

Edward asked innocently, 'What is it when the lawyer does it with a client?'

'Tortuous?' They investigated that, and left the Foundation in the living room until morning.

Frances extracted a complete accounting of Julia's remarks from Eddie with the ease of a lawyer whose witness had ingested truth serum. When he was emptied of all that was said, Frances asked for his own thoughts. 'She may be right about closing the Foundation. To date the books have been largely unnoticed. Even those which were published by text-book houses are not very wonderful, and the stuff from our own press is more deadly than almost everything else in the market.'

'I heard that proprietary 'our' as a modifier for the word press.'

Eddie had to think about that. But finally he agreed that he felt proprietary. First because he'd accepted a Fellowship, and more, because Dr T had had the right idea about writing history and about thinking historically. 'It's a worthless thing to do if you don't do it right!'

Frances walked to the window. She had a vision forming of their life together. Of their future. Therefore she asked, 'And do I get it that you will hang in until the matter of Bernard's competence is sorted out?' She had to know, because the answer determined how she should imagine their future.

Eddie drew the pause out as long as he dared, thinking furiously: get in a fight for power? write his book in peace? Write the Tscherbateff book? Apply for a professorship at Yale? Find a real job the way Newt Gingrich did?

As Frances stood still at the window, Eddie had time to spin variations on all these ideas. When he swallowed to prepare for speaking, he thought he was about to say a good deal. What he actually said was, 'Yes.'

'Fine. I can live with that, and it will be good for you! Now, it's my experience that where there is money, there's power playing. Any going on within the campus?'

Surprised at the turn of topic, Eddie said, 'No question. But just mild tugs, even between Bernard and Dr T until he was killed. And goes on still between all the Resident Fellows and Bernard.'

'And what does Bernard do to keep control?'

Eddie thought for a minute, 'Sorry, I hadn't asked myself that. But yes, he runs the whole place with intimidation, the curled lip of scorn. Short reins. The same way he flattens everyone's prose. Everyone but me, and, I guess Dr Randall, the Byzantine.'

Frances wanted Byzantine explained, but decided to keep Eddie on the track, so instead she asked what, if anything, else went on behind the scenes.

Suppressing memories of Pinky wheedling and flaunting to stay in the limelight, 'Sure, like any little court, but I was never in the loop, and I'm sure not now. But nothing much that I ever saw. Bernard is straight-laced. Very stiff. Hard to imagine him involved .'

'Think! Money? Influence?'

'Well, lots of money. Something like three or four hundred million. Bernard has the spending of the income at his sole discretion.'

'Chances are, that's it. But why give anyone that much power?'

'I only know that's how Leila Armbruster wanted it, so that her husband, Dr Tscherbateff, had leeway. Total control of the money and scholarships.' Eddie shook his head, 'Woman of principle. If she gave power to her husband, he could give it to his successor.'

Frances turned her attention to the Trustees. Who were they, and what did he know of how Bernard got on with them.

'How would I know? We never get anything from Bernard, and when the Trustees come to Santa Barbara they eat at one table, and we eat at another. Rather stiff, and not the way Dr T did it, but Bernard likes it. And I know the Trustees follow the assets carefully, because I hear that sort of conversation; very self-satisfied! You'd think they were talking about their own money. And Bernard reports every penny each month; I just don't think that's a problem.'

Frances waited for Eddie to go on, sitting quietly, yellow pad and pencil in hand. She was moved just by the base rumble of his voice; what's a base with color? Bassatura?

'Well, here's the Trustees. Bernard and Julia, of course. A rich and elderly attorney named Fingle-something. A skinny older woman*, very expensive looking, who comes in her own limo, usually with Fingle-whoosis; Mrs Bull by name. Dr Ansen-Mollern, former president of the University, Bill Capshaw the electronics whiz. That's six. Oh, and the one guy who is almost a buddy. Jamison Barker.'

Frances invited more information about Barker.

Barker, she learned, was an entrepreneur who backed movies, sporting events, explorations and anything else exciting from the deep bags of loot left him by his various relatives. Everyone named Barker who died seemed to leave it all to Jamison Barker. Some Jamisons seemed to do the same. A thoroughly nice type, Eddie declared. 'I met him riding our back trails. He plays polo, but likes a free ride, and uses the three horses we keep at the Foundation. He likes my Morgan, and we often go out the morning before Board Meetings. At first I couldn't get why he stayed on the Trustees, because everything else he does is high risk, high action. Fast. But he has another side. The same guy that likes polo likes a leisurely ride, and he sees history books as the slow pace that points up the rest of his life. Very well read, and thoughtful.'

'Is he a potential ally?

Eddie thought so, and agreed to call Barker when he got to Santa Barbara. Then Eddie did some back-pedaling. Bernard wasn't so bad, he explained; downright fatherly sometimes. Julia was excessively critical; inherited position had perhaps gone to her head. Julia was asking him to go over his boss' head, or at least around him. To tattle-tale.

* *She is Cindy Achterarder Bull, who appears in HOW TO BECOME A BILLIONAIRE*

'You can't duck responsibility! You know something is wrong, and have the authority from the Chair to find out what it is!'

'I write about history, I don't make it, nor even want to! This isn't some lawsuit you can make come out any way you want it to.'

'Mrs Vickery says you write excellent history! All the more compelling reason to get in there and slug it out! And, damn it, lawsuits don't come out any way I want them to! No more than your histories do!'

'My writing is just popular drivel. Honest. Sure, I tell it the way it was, and if I can't figure how it was, I write all sides of the possible conclusions. But what Julia thinks about it is nothing but flattery. Just being nice.'

Frances proceeded to read the riot act. Female version, strengthened by forensic training and a voice getting louder by the paragraph.

Not one to stand for undignified treatment, Eddie grabbed his coat and walked out.

She was waiting at the United terminal at Kennedy Airport when he got there the next morning.

Frances first question was about the Villa del Torre, where the Foundation was housed. 'I want to visualize you there.'

Edward Hamilton was dazed. 'What about last night?'

'Nothing,' she said, 'Nothing but noise. Didn't mean anything.'

'Did too! Fried the hell out of me!' And lost a whole night with you, he added to himself.

'Well, I admit I was stupid, because I had to sleep alone, with the other three condoms on the table next to me. It didn't give me any pleasure, I admit!' Frances laughed the open way she had.

Eddie said, 'Women!' and added that he couldn't live without them, nor could he apparently live with this one. Instead of prolonging the exchange, he walked her into the Red Carpet Room and laid out the estate on a napkin.

'It is the Armbruster Estate, a big spread in the foothills of Montecito. Like a Spanish town. The big house has only two main bedrooms, and six servant's rooms. At one corner is a tower, something on the scale of a big church tower, except that this one holds water. Six stories seem enormous next to a one storied house, high as it is. Then in back, towards the view, a long lawn with cottages on either side. Dr T's place was along there. Then a fancy garden down some steps, the big swimming pool, and beyond, more recent cottages, built by the Foundation for newer resident Fellows. I had one of those umm, when I was married. Over here towards the public road, kitchen gardens, staff houses, and a stable and tack rooms, with some corrals. Nice. In fact, beautiful.'

'Mmm. Sounds like Bernard does himself rather proud.'

'Not. He lives in two dinky rooms, and Pinky has another, in the old servant's quarters. The main bedroom is for visitors or for Mrs Vickery. The other main bedroom is all computers and research hook-ups to the University of California, and thence, by modem, to the rest of the library world. Even the Library of Congress.'

Their attention passed to departures, warm kisses, and promises to call as soon as possible. Eddie felt happy as he boarded, and Frances had the feeling of being in love as she watched him go.

Waiting on the runway, Eddie thought, 'How can it be? On Sunday I'm in Ireland. On Monday I fall in love, on Tuesday I'm in my lover's bed, on Wednesday I'm so pissed off that I never want to see the pushy broad again, Thursday

I'm off to California alone, and hating it! How's that for the history of the world?

3

SANTA BARBARA

Edward walked through the dark spaces of the entrance hall, and out onto the blinding light of California's noon sun. He shaded his hand to look out towards the Pacific, dotted with oil platforms, but gleaming seductively even so. Closer, the immaculate lawns of the immediate garden of the Villa, and closer still, his former wife, lying on a chaise. My God, he thought, she needs help to sit up! Pinky had grown several sizes, apparently all in the breasts. What had seemed formidable to a scholar with a new doctorate, were now basketballs! Awesome! And odd!

Although he had thought 'sitting up' in the symbolic sense, it appeared applicable in the actual sense as well. Pinky was smashed!

'Well, Daddy said you were coming! Cute Ned! Let's start over again, how about it?' She waved her hand as though inviting several persons to tennis or tea.

'Hello Pinky. See you later, have to find my room.'

Edward retreated, ducked into the office, formerly the gunroom of the estate. Mrs Loesch, the housekeeper and senior staff member rose when he came in, stretched her arms, and surprised him with the kiss of a fond aunt. 'You are in Dr Randall's cottage. Not done over yet, but you'll like it better than being in the main house.

To reach that bungalow, on the west side of the lawn and about half way to the swimming pool's sunken garden, he'd have to pass Pinky again.

Instead, he sought Bernard in the grand Venetian-style library that served as his office. In the outer office, Mrs Wells, secretary to Dr Tscherbateff, had passed seamlessly into the service of Dr Esbenshade, but she hadn't liked it. At one time she had made Edward a confidant as to what she disliked about Bernard. Edward had firmly cut all that off, saying the equivalent of not to bite the hand which... Edward had said it all so well that Mrs Wells now worshipped him, and though she did not confide any longer, she always let him know she had things to say.

Hugs and greetings completed, she rang Bernard to announce him.

'Oh, I'd think not,' Bernard said when he heard Edward's request. 'I'm doing everything to keep you pointed in the direction of your own book. Brilliant exposition! Probably the most important work the Foundation has under way.'

'And that is the sole reason you did not relay Mrs Vickery's message to me?'

'Of course. Although I have made it a policy to discourage communication 'around me' as one might say. Nothing personal, of course, but it really wouldn't do to have the Fellows dealing with the Trustees. Oh, and how did Mrs Vickery's interest get through to you?' Bernard strutted on through an obfuscatory forest.

At last, Edward cut in, 'Well, Mrs Vickery has asked me to write the book, and asked that I take a detour to do it.'

Bernard looked out the tall French window for a time, then said, 'No matter how noble, it shouldn't be allowed, dear boy. They want puffery, not history; any hack could do what she wants. You're too good for it. Still, I owe you careful consideration; see me tomorrow. Oh, and we dine in tonight.'

Dining in. A Tscherbateff tradition that a fine meal would provoke high thoughts, wit and insights into the events of the week. In his day, dining in did just that. Dark suit until Thanksgiving, then dinner jackets through Twelfth Night, then dark suits again. Edward remembered how much fun that was when Dr T conducted the dinners; winter dress up always meant outside ladies included. Lots of laughter, real camaraderie. That rarest of all feeling among men, collegiality. Mutual respect, shared interests, common goals. Yawning differences that heightened the pleasure each took in his colleagues.

Walking down to his cottage, he saw Pinky's chair had been vacated. How could that poor child have spun me around her finger? I must have imagined that she loved me! The capacity for self-deception among the young! No, among anyone, where the opposite sex is involved.

He glanced at the cottage, opposite his own, which replaced the one destroyed in the explosion which had killed Dr T. A careful replica of the original. Bernard's love of the Villa showed in the quality of the replacement.

Edward unpacked, remembering that this cottage had been Dr Randall's for years. It was clean, but still marked with his missing books, and the worn spots where he'd brushed by the wall, or touched a door thousands of times. Not a word that Dr Randall was in residence at the Foundation, and that made Edward uneasy. Randall's 'Procopius and the Secret Histories' was the exception among books from the Foundation. It was brilliantly phrased and full of insights. Had it not been about an obscure phase of Byzantium's decadence, it would have had a National Booksellers Award.

Bitterly, Edward reflected that Randall's book had escaped emasculation because no one cared a rat's ass about Byzantium. That was probably the reason, that his own work was received without correction or emendation.

In the several hours left of the afternoon, Eddie met Jamison Barker on the beach in front of the Miramar. They jogged up to Fernald Point, then back down to the cliff which blocks East Beach from Butterfly Beach. Walking back, Eddie laid out the reasons for his trip, and his worries that all was not right on campus, specifically with Bernard.

Barker took it all in, and laughed. 'Shit, you must be the biggest turkey in all academia! You're being groomed. One more book as big as your last one, and you're international! Stature of the two Beards or Barbara Tuchman!'

Eddie cringed because, for quite different reason, neither was highly regarded among historians, the team being polemical and the other too popular. Eddie prepared a defense of Barbara, whom he admired tremendously, and dropped it to listen to Barker.

'No Edward, Bernard's an ass, but he's our ass, and I think all the money undoubtedly dribbled away is worth it when we get one Edward Hamilton and one Arthur Randall. And I have high hopes for Medina. And the Middletons, though God knows they need an editor!'

Eddie wasn't sold, so Barker volunteered. 'The main thing I have against Bernard is the way he pampers your ex-wife. She's a slut, and if he can't put a cork in her, he ought to lock her up! Ke-rist! Last week she had some screaming fit right on campus.'

'Poor Pinky.'

'Poor Pinky my ass! She was contracted to Lyman Ellis, hot-shot megamerger type. Bernard told me with great satisfaction; like he'd achieved his life's dream! Some engagement. No sooner than she had a ring, ugly big emerald like a 'GO' light, than Lyman catches her doing a standing fuck on the hips of the towel boy at the Beach Club. I guess Lyman was pretty cool about it, but not Pinky. Still hanging on to the kid, who'd lost it by then I'd guess, she bawled Lyman out for sneaking around. Then she threw her ring at him, and somehow he didn't catch it. Bang! Ninety-five thousand of emerald shattered like glass. Staff spent hours sweeping up emerald spears!' He laughed.

Eddie felt very low, and humiliated. For Pinky and for himself, and he liked Barker less for having told him all this.

'Well, buck up. Lyman is suing her for the value of the ring "obtained on the false promises and misrepresentations!" I hear Bernard is prepared to settle in full. His own money, right out of what I'd guess is a shallow pocket.'

Eddie started to jog again, unwilling to hear more.

Later, as dusk approached, Edward looked from the cottage back towards the house to see the mountains looming behind the slopes of the tile roof, by the water tower, glowing with the reflected rays of sunset. Too many trees here in the heart of the garden to see the ocean, and sundown came rapidly. Sunlight replaced by chill.

A little cool, he lit the gas logs in the shallow fireplace, and began to change for dinner. Too early. He sat to read, but dropped the book. 'Frances' he said aloud. Missing her, angry that he was here without her, he dialed his code, and then dialed her in New York. And spoke urgently of his love and need. She responded in similar terms, but made no promises.

When he hung up, he sat in the gathering darkness, aware that he'd started a difficult bit of work. And he wasn't sure why. He had no great need to reform or purify the Foundation, but he'd be willing to see it done. But he felt silly merely to relay impressions or detail to Julia Vickery. And somehow, he didn't think Frances would think that was quite enough for him to do.

Why should Frances care? He was as in love with her as he knew how to be; did she reciprocate? He had no way of knowing. But, maybe, if he sorted out matters at the Foundation, she'd see him as a man of action. A man she might prefer to an historian!

Gathered in the great living room, all the resident Fellows, a scattering of wives, and Pinky awaited him. And Jamison Barker. Pinky still awash, or again awash? Cordial greetings, a knowing wink of congratulation, a solemn handclasp, an abrazo. Each Fellow had a special acknowledgment. 'Am I so welcome a sight? I don't see why you all missed me so much!'

They had missed him, and welcomed him home. Pinky demonstrably, kissing him with one leg flung out behind, and her enormous boobs cutting off his breath. Pneumatic, he decided, not flesh as he remembered them.

Barker kept carefully on the far side of the room, watching, but apparently interested only in some scholar's chatter about computer access to Library of Congress catalogs.

Dinner, four courses, two wines and port, was jovial. The scholars on holiday from Bernard's decorum. Edward told Irish stories, Dr Medina embellished with Iberian versions of the same, and even Dr Randall, present despite Edward's misgivings, had three ports, and sang a Cambridge song so obscure that no one knew at what part to take offense.

Three stalwarts. Medina, the distinguished student of parliaments, the French Estates General and Regional, the Cortes of Castile, of England and the various convocations and councils of the Mother Church; a specialist in how meetings debated and shifted allegiances and leadership. Dignified, Spanish, and a horseman who had spent many hours with Edward on the mountain trails behind Santa Barbara.

Randall, a youngish seventy who practiced shiatsu on the lawns at six of every morning, and bumbled gently through each day. The most arresting writer of the Fellows, and the only one not badgered by Bernard Esbenshade. His subject? The decline of the Eastern Empire: Byzantium. He made it vital, as no one else might have done.

Where Medina, a widower, and Randall, never married, worked with monkish zeal, Dr and Mrs Middleton worked as a comfortable team. They held a Fellowship between them. Their interest was the growth of the United States as an economic entity. Their early works were widely read, if not very interestingly written. Under Bernard's baleful pruning, their uninspired prose had become almost indecipherable. Laden with graphs, necessarily using language fraught with trade terms, no publisher had touched them for years. They were the Foundation's most prolific authors, and most costly publications.

The stalwarts separately and in gangs, had once asked Edward for help in repelling Bernard's control of their work. Each, feeling in some way, that less editing and more collegial input would be desirable, and each crediting Edward with more influence than he believed he had. Tonight the stalwarts were as approving as doting grandparents. It made him a little edgy.

Pinky made obvious passes at Edward during dinner, but other than that, she allowed him to chat with colleagues before and at the dinner table. But over coffee in the living room, she pled her own case. 'I was just too young to know what I was throwing away! I wish we could start over! I really need someone like you. I mean, so that I can keep growing up.'

Out. Growing out; Edward tried to breathe air not tainted with brandy and cigarette smoke, to breathe around her, so to speak. 'This has been a big welcome home, but truly, Pinky, we've had it. No good. But thanks anyway.'

This was not well received. Pinky spoke what to her was a simple truth, and spoke it loudly. 'You are a shit-face!' She made a fast exit, carrying the brandy bottle. 'I'll get you!' she said softly as she whirled past.

Startled scholars folded around the coffee-pouring Mrs Middleton, and Bernard began a long diatribe against the LA Times to a bemused Dr Medina, who had not seen the attack coming.

'Not, I think, a good description of you, old chap.' Dr Randall looked up at Edward. 'Not to worry. These things pass, even with Miss Esbenshade. She just hates rejection. Temper getting worse, too.'

'Thanks. You know, I was worried about you. Not being in your cottage, I mean.'

'Ever so politely, Dr Esbenshade has been hinting that I allow repairs to be made. Now I can't be disturbed because of a little painting or a leaky tap, so I've just dug in my heels. Non disturbari, as it were, you see.'

'Then why?'

'He asked me to yield to you. Of course, for you I was pleased to shift to Bungalow B. I hope you like it, but you know, I don't believe I vamoosed fast enough! They haven't even started re-working the place, have they?'

Randall spoke as though Edward had intended to stay at Villa del Torre. Not kind to correct the old boy about that. Ask Bernard tomorrow.

Barker kept his distance, but it came to Edward that Barker had troubled to come for dinner to support him, and he forgave what was said on the beach. The men banged each other's shoulders and said good night, planning to meet at the stables in the morning.

He came back to the shabby cottage cold, tired and slightly damp from walking down the lawn. The kind of night when he'd ordinarily put on the gas logs. But he shuddered, thinking of Dr T, and piled on a layer of sweaters, and dived under the blankets.

He wakened, later, gasping, disoriented, and so sleepy he couldn't focus on the sound of the phone. Reached for it, fell plumb out of the sack. Head cleared, layer of cold air, faintly moldy from the carpet. Got to evacuate. Gas up there at bed level. Scamper to door in a crawl. Christ, place'll blow up, like Dr Ts.

In the garden. Phone still ringing in the cottage. Mist on ground, cool, not cold like Ireland. Clearing head, retching. Thought cleared; must prevent explosion. Sweater in bird bath. Does wet cloth help as in a fire? Supported by doorframe, falling to a crawl to the fireplace, half a mile in, reached for the key to the gas jet. None. Exit. Water heater closet pried open, doused pilot. Then, going in by the bathroom door to the patio, dropped to the floor, reached around the door with comprehension, turned off the key to the gas jet. Damn gas jet had been turned on to kill him!

He dragged himself to the lower patio, rolled into a lawn chair and slept.

Dr Middleton wakened him. 'Not you? Taking these mind pills? Good gracious…'

'Nothing. Think there was a gas leak in Randall's cottage.'

'You're there? Thought it was being rebuilt.'

'No, I have it while I'm here.' Edward struggled upright.

'Something the matter with the cottage?'

'No, nothing like that. Perfectly cozy all these years, until, suddenly, when you came, Bernard evicted Randall. Must commence the repairs at once. Something about fiscal periods, expenditure during, you see.'

Then Bernard had anticipated trouble. No accident. He expected to use the cover of an old and obsolete cottage to murder the putative biographer of Dr. Tscherbateff! Nothing clearer!

The fresh air had eased the work of Edward's lungs, and except for a monumental headache, nothing seemed to be wrong. Well, not noticing dizziness, and bouts of nausea.

'There's Dr Hamilton's cottage,' he heard a voice. And another, Frances' 'Here I am, faithful to your command!'

'Christ, I asked you to come, and did you call me a couple of hours ago? Early AM?'

'From Denver, transferring for here. To let you know I was coming, and ask directions.'

Edward folded her into his arms, 'Saved my fool life!' And he told her how and why. And asked, 'Now what? Guess I have to see him about my contract. Or better, I'll throw the whole thing in his face. Damn gas jet didn't go on by itself!'

'The same accident as Dr Tscherbateff had? Ridiculous; there aren't coincidences.'

'Probably not. Dr T's accident put someone in mind of this little effort. Bernard never had an original thought in his head, so he's the most likely to have staged this.' Edward tried his legs, found them steady, and added, 'If he's that desperate to kill the Tscherbateff biography, well, there's something very wrong here.'

Looking over the cottage, they found a bent coat hanger in the bathroom. They experimented with it. It would pull the key on, several tries proved it. A killer never need come into the bedroom at all. Just lie low, and reach two feet around the corner. Inspection showed the door from the patio to the bathroom had shrunk in its' frame until no sound was made from the friction of opening it, or closing it, for that matter. No premeditation showing from the door.

Barker came around the corner, tired of waiting at the stable. Appalled at what he heard. 'Knew you needed protection. Kerist! Oh, sorry. You'd be Frances?'

Felling a tad better, Eddie rang for three breakfast trays please, and crisp toast, lots, and thank you.

Frances had a yellow pad on her lap, the lawyer's response to anything. 'He's like the Wizard of Oz. Everyone thinks he can do anything. My attitude is that we take Frank Morgan's role seriously. Both of us charge in there, ask for the miracle, then the fair Dorothy carries the day.'

'What? You made that up!' Eddie almost smiled.

Barker roared.

'Cross the chest cavity, did not!' Frances laughed as Eddie did just that.

'That's blackmail! Oh! The Wizard of Oz. You're shameless.' Eddie paused, about to quote author and date of publication. Instead he said, 'And Toto threatens to bark if a Toto-sized golden parachute isn't forthcoming.'

Barker roared again, 'Eddie, that's the first time I have ever heard you be funny! Frances is bringing out the best in you. Next you'll sing like old Randall.'

Eddie was a little cross, because he'd told jokes at dinner the night before. Barker had too much cleverness, Eddie thought.

But Frances agreed with Barker. 'It's true. I'm trying to lighten him up a bit!

When Eddie and Francis walked up to the house, a maid handed Eddie a Call Slip. Would he return the call of Jack Tscherbateff? But first things first.

They presented themselves on the Kirman rug, directly in front of Bernard's vast Charles Tenth desk.

'My dear Edward! I was so worried! And so relieved when Dr Middleton told me that no harm had been done!'

Not wasting words, Eddie asked, 'Why are the Tscherbateff and Armbruster heirs after me?'

'Oh, just the biography. I turned them off. No point in interrupting a work as important as yours; you just can't waste your talent. And they are spoiled people, and want what they want. I can screen you from them. I saw that young Jack called you this morning. He's a time waster. I'll return the call, if you like.'

Bernard had been avoiding Frances, not sure who she was nor why, and addressing Edward fist.

Eddie finally introduced her, 'Frances Russell, my attorney.'

He seemed pleased to see them, not a shadow of any reaction beyond good morning to an attractive woman.

'Sorry, Bernard, I want to do the book. Dr T had ideas, methods and principles that would help us all to remember. I'm going to peel more from his correspondence, his articles, and distill from both books.'

A pause, during which Bernard seemed to measure the size of the Kirman.

Eddie knew the effect of silence; it's unsettling to an adversary. Vague office sounds filtered in, the distant voices of the Mexican garden staff. The phrase 'in for the kill' came to mind;

he'd committed himself to Julia's purpose. Been driven to it by this worm.

Finally, Bernard spoke, 'I was at first disinclined to allow it under the terms of your Fellowship. For the best reasons: you are too valuable. But I've thought about it, seriously. And discussed it with our colleagues.'

Which Eddie knew was a valueless comment; the Fellows thought exactly as Bernard allowed them to think. 'Miss Russell represents me, and I wish to go over matters in the light of my near asphyxiation last night. I perceive that I am not welcome, in your eyes, to take up the bio of Dr T. So unwelcome that you attempted to finish me off; close my book before the first chapter.'

Bernard cocked his head, as an indulgent grandfather might, listening to a silly and imaginative child.

Frances spoke. 'And that, sir, leads us to our proposal. All is forgotten, provided my client, Dr Hamilton, returns to Ireland, first to write the desired biography of Dr Tscherbateff in his own way, and then to complete the The Effects of Popular Beliefs Upon the Course of a People.' She consulted her handbag, looked up and added, 'Which you will agree is now to be called, Deadly History.'

Bernard leaned forward, a bland expression canceling out his ferret-like smile. 'All this is nothing. My colleague Edward and I can settle these misunderstandings, and we won't need to run up legal bills. We can amend his Fellowship contract right here.'

Bernard rose, circled the desk, and said, 'Not that there was the slightest doubt in my mind, once I thought it over, that Edward could do both. Mustn't be impatient, son.' Bernard touched Edward slightly on the shoulder as he walked out of the room to speak to his secretary. And to terminate further conversation. 'Until luncheon,' he remarked, by way of exit line.

'Hard to believe anything when he's such a smooth actor.' Frances said.

'Gregory IX,' Eddie said, committing an historigraphical error: never infer from the similar behavior of two persons that they are like each other!

Lunch was served in the usual style of the Foundation. A groaning buffet with the makings of sandwiches, and a tureen of soup. Warm to compliment a Fall day. And fruit. And starched linen, fine country-style plates, a half-acre of silver implements. Iced tea in tankard mounted on a gimbal. Buttermilk, milk and non-fat blue, each in it's own crystal pitcher. Attended by ten resident Fellows, each carefully dressed in dated-casual styles; blazers, slacks, turtlenecks or Ascots in polo shirts. A set piece, taken altogether.

Again, Jamison Barker stood in the background, away from Edward, but watchful.

'So sorry about this morning, Edward.' Dr Randall stood next to Frances, squinting slightly against the glare from the window. 'Condensation absolutely rots metal pipes. I've seen it before in the sprinklers, and awful, in Dr Ts cottage, too.'

Memory flooded back. Two-thirty in the morning, the night Dr T blew up, Bernard going up the path ahead of him. 'Egregious ass!' Edward startled Dr Randall, then said, 'Sorry, I meant myself!' He'd been looking for Pinky, and Bernard has just come from turning on the gas at Dr Ts. Edward put down his soup spoon, and looked along the table at Bernard, who was scolding a Dr Rassmusson about subjunctives, use of same, and desirable avoidance in the past tense.

Bernard saw Edward's look, but continued blandly, not even sneaking a second glance to see if Edward's look contained anything beyond anger. Edward felt pressure on his loafer; Frances said, 'Stop that,' and smiled a party smile, saying afterwards, 'Don't glare.'

Eddie answered her with some heat. 'Deadly History! Where'd you get that one? Sounds like a whodunit. Won't do.'

Frances simply smiled, for she knew the title was thoroughly commercial.

When the table rose, Elizabeth Wells, Bernard's secretary detained Edward. 'The Director would like to say good bye to you, and tells me to say that the draft is ready for you to examine in the ante-office, just here if you please.' Mrs Wells looked quite pleased about something.

Edward squared his shoulders, and went towards the Director's office, motioning with his hand for Frances not to come. Barker paid no attention, and followed right on in to the great library, almost as an escort, walking like a royal consort, three paces to the rear.

'Now Edward, I said I'm very pleased with your work. In fact, I wish to recognize that you are our leading scholar. Thus, your contract is even now being revised to designate you Senior Fellow, the first such honor I have bestowed.'

'Cut the...' Edward began, becoming angry. But the Fellows began to file in, until Edward understood that an informal reception was being mounted for the occasion of his creation! Good academic manners counseled him to stand still. But he felt far from senior to these men; embarrassed in fact! The whole thing was so unfair to the others, that for the moment, he forgot to pursue his anger that this stuffed shirt had killed Dr T.

The passing of port and biscuit prolonged the agony. When the whole round of handshaking and compliments was over, but before the scholars had left, Bernard grasped his hand, leaned into Edwards' space as far as his ear, saying, '...and the compensation is substantially more, as well!' Bernard then backed off to say, 'And so good-bye!'

Barker collared him, and practically frog-marched him out into the driveway where Eddie's suitcase and Frances' garment bag were already in the car. 'Whew. I was afraid you'd have a fit of plain speaking in there. Blown it.'

Frances had been right behind Barker, and made a similar comment as soon as she caught up to what had happened. 'Damn it, I connived at blackmail! That's what I did. That F-ing bastard pulled the same stunt on Dr T, and I saw him practically coming out of Dr T's cottage. And I'm so stupid that I didn't figure it out until today! But oh yes, he saw me look at him. That's when he invented Senior Fellow, and thought up a raise. I should have quit but those good old boys really thought I earned it! How can I be proud of it?'

Barker assured him that the Senior Fellowship had been discussed before, and he, Barker, was heartily in favor of it. And delighted that Bernard had made, for a change, a fast decision. '...because I thought he'd drag the process out like a sentence by who's-your-uncle?'

'Edward Gibbon, ' Frances supplied for Barker. Then said, 'Relax Eddie. I've checked you out.'

Edward asked, 'Checked me?' They got into Barker's Rolls and drove down the long drive to the public road. 'Oh, I adore you and all that, but I had no handle on your academic standing.' Frances laughed her throaty way.

Disgruntled, Eddie answered, 'Ya, and now you know I don't teach, and I hole up in celibate corners of the world and write stuff no one reads. Though libraries order it; must be a flaw in the education they give librarians.'

'Shh. You know what Harvard says? The foremost historian in the country: you! Moreover you have the two historic titles in the country that are selling!'

'Yes, and Yale says I write too much'

'No actually, Dr Seligman said you are prolific, and thank god, because you have it all to say. You deserved the promotion, and the pay.'

Barker said, 'Ya. Your modesty is sounding too thin. You looking for more praise or a kick in the butt? She can do the first, and I'll do the latter, so just choose.'

They rolled into the motor court of the Biltmore Hotel, where Edward and Frances were received with the gladness that an hotel staff saves for those arriving in Rolls Royces.

Barker said good-bye, call him any time, and his car purred away.

A surfer, rangy , but not so tall. Bleached, blonde and happy, Jack Tscherbateff sat in a deep chair in the Biltmore's bar. He didn't look so much out of place, as uninterested in luxuries such as the hotel provided.

'Diet coke is fine. Look, Julia is always on about the purpose of the Foundation. It's not that I don't care, but I have no idea what it's about. My IQ is about thirty, and Dad did all the thinking our family needed.'

'You graduated from Stanford. That's not stupid.' Frances, always thorough, had checked.

Edward added, '...so I'd say you aren't motivated.'

Jack brushed the hair from his forehead. 'Right. Whatever.'

'Jack, I'm going to write a biography of your father. In it, I'm bringing back to life his ideals and dreams for the Foundation. Leila's dreams too. Those meant something to you, didn't they?'

'Look, they did what they wanted, and Leila was more mother to me than my own ever was able to be. I loved them both, and I'm endlessly grateful, too. You know, Dad left me all he had, a few hundred thousand dollars. What do you guess Leila did for me? Ten, believe it, million. Dollars man!' He edged forward in his chair. I care!' And then he slid back, slouching, 'But I can't do anything about it. Not a damn thing.'

'You can, you know. You have every right to be on campus, have meals there. Just do it. Make friends with some of the scholars, even the Fellows. Watch what goes on, make your own judgements.'

Jack knew the buxom Pinky. Had tried her once himself, though he had no intention of thinking about it in the presence of her ex! He saw her in all the local bars. Fair game, but he resisted much traveled roads. Even so, he'd played 'what if' when he saw her. Not much to recommend going up to the Foundation to be bored and, finally, frustrated. 'Why…'

Edward took a deep breath. 'Would you help us if I could show that your father was murdered? That the explosion was no accident?' To that moment, Eddie had no intention of doing any such thing. He'd seen himself as merely a reporter, an historian of current events. Now he'd committed himself to an active investigation. He saw Frances' eyes widen. Approvingly, he thought.

Jack tucked his legs up, and tears formed at the edges of his widened eyes. 'Killed?'

'I think I have it, but not down cold, but there's a lot of work to do. But I need your help.'

'Count on it,' Jack said, putting out a wide brown hand.

Montecito is an unincorporated area within Santa Barbara County. Fires, their out-putting and causes of, are dealt with by the Montecito Fire District, a Santa Barbara County entity.

Edward pursued the matter-of-fact Captain Joe Martin for information about the explosion of two years before.

'Definitely caused by an accumulation of natural gas. The structure exploded from the top. Gas rises, and when it ignites, the lid comes off, so to speak. That's the way the cottage went up.'

Edward asked several ways if the investigators were satisfied that the whole thing was accidental.

'Now wait. We do a thorough job of evaluating these things. I don't say we're always right, but there has been nothing to make us wrong about the incident at the Foundation until you started asking questions. So what do you want it to be? And what have you got that would make us re-evaluate our finding?'

Eddie demurred. No facts, only a motive which could do more damage than good if revealed. 'Just asking how you do it, that's all.' He felt foolish, and apparently Captain Martin saw it too.

'Look. Let's go over it all again, and you ask questions as we go. First there's the age of the cottage. Then there's some corrosion of the pipes. I'd like to have found the exact length of pipe that leaked, and I was surprised that we didn't. But looking at these other pieces of gas pipe, well, several are near to perforating and leaking. They'd mostly smell before they did any damage. But somehow, this particular leak didn't. Probably no one smelled the leak because it was so near the flue of the chimney. It just vented up the flue, we think. Probably went on for a long time until that night. Then maybe an increase in gas pressure in the mains. Not supposed to happen, but can, and a little more flaking of the deteriorating metal, and a little more wind pressure at the top of the flue. Bad prescription, but that's about how it had to happen. If, as you ask, it was an accident.'

Once more, Eddie re-lived the explosion, the dust of which took several hours to disperse. From the first moments, the broken bundle of striped bathrobe was clearly of Dr Tscherbateff. The French windows of his bed room angled outward, kept from falling only by their lower hinges, Through this opening, the body had been partly pushed, restrained by a tangle of bed-covers and pillows. The roofless cottage, the loss of that fine man, the destruction… Eddie remembered sheets of writing paper scattered in the garden. Pages of notes about Douglas Southall Freeman's treatment of George Washington. Staff and Fellows had tried to gather these last evidences of Dr T. Put in order, the good man was trying to understand why so brilliant an historian as Freeman had reported General Washington as though he were a Victorian man with a rather Presbyterian attitude! Dr T had pursued the thought, and was developing a critical method to test whether a writer was unconsciously putting his mind and life into the analysis of other ages.

Edward allowed his mind to drift, until Captain Martin shuffled the open file together again. 'Now look, Dr Hamilton, we're available and interested. You can come in as often as you like, ask what you like, and we're glad to see you.' And he held his hand out in a kindly dismissal.

Eddie felt he'd accomplished nothing.

Before Frances and Eddie left Montecito, the stalwarts came down to the Biltmore for lunch: the two Drs Middleton, and Drs Randall and Medina. On the patio, facing the Pacific Ocean, the air was warm, the breeze polite, and food and wine of a quality to turn harder heads than the academics who sat with Frances.

In a low voice, Edward outlined what he meant to do with the biography. Tangentially he said he would document and explain how the Foundation's current standards of historiography were below the Founders' standards, and who was to blame for the situation.

Middleton got it first. Didn't like it. 'Bernard's an ass, but he's sincere. Just that he's over his head. He holds down a one-room schoolhouse and imagines it's a great university!'

'Look, I have nothing against Bernard other than something very bad he once did. Which, were it known, none of you would forgive. This book is another thing. I'm out to create a goal for historians, and to explain a method for reaching that goal.'

'Strategy, Edward. Takes strategies to reach goals, not methods. Use methods to create to strategies.'

Dr Medina had another set of words, and the four academics fell to wrangling over how one tautologically reached a goal. Edward let them discuss it, waiting for their attention to return to what he was saying, as it finally did. The return to Edward's theme faltered, however, on what he'd said about Bernard doing something bad.

Randall looked carefully at Eddie. Speculatively. 'Be careful! Things may be more complex than you think. Webs inside webs, you see.'

'Nonsense.' said the female Dr Middleton. 'Bernard doesn't have evil in him. I can't support making a fool of him, but I can't say that educating him would be a bad thing!'

Eddie said, 'If I'm right, believe me, you will want me to do as I intend to do. In any case, the biography will be educational, and that may be all there is to it. Now let me ask you, did anyone know in advance that I'd be made a Senior Fellow?'

'Bernard told me when we walked in to lunch. Said keep it mum, but be sure to be in his office right after lunch.'

Middleton confirmed that. 'So?'

'I think he decided that I'd be promoted when he found I wasn't killed by the potential explosion in my cottage.'

'Dr T!' the older men said, almost together.

Eddie said what sounded like 'Zactly!'

Back in the blue cold of New York, Eddie and Frances called again on Julia. They explained what had happened in Santa Barbara. And outlined Eddie's belief that Bernard Esbenshade had caused the explosion which killed Dr Tscherbateff, as well as that intended to kill him.

'He had motive in both cases, and was near Dr T's cottage at the right time. Whether I can prove anything more remains to be seen.'

Julia held her hands before her face, blacking out the vision that Edward had aroused. That of her stepfather flung into the air, smashed by the force of the explosion. 'He didn't deserve that,' she said after a few moments. Then, straightening her already-perfect gray hair, Julia said that she wished she hadn't known.

'Sorry, we don't know, we can surmise, but nothing beyond that.'

'I had shied away from bringing Bernard down. A bad precedent, I'd thought. Now? And I'm sure Edward is right! Bernard is as good as out! Will the police take over now?'

'Julia! Please wait! Dr T's principle was that you can not reason from incomplete data, or make conclusions from similar events that may in fact be unrelated. Of all the reasons not to attack Bernard, Dr Ts are the most compelling!'

Julia conceded that Edward was right. Reluctantly. 'Then what should I do?'

Frances interjected, 'Eddie is concerned that he's being paid off as in blackmail. You see, no sooner had Eddie escaped the effort to gas him, or blow him up, whichever it was, than Dr Esbenshade made him a Senior Fellow!'

'Grand! And I am delighted that the first historian to be honored that way would be you!'

'There's more, Bernard also increased Eddie's monthly check, and expanded the contract to include the book you want done!'

'Grand again! Just what I wanted. Congratulations Edward!' Julia hugged him, and added, 'It is not a pay-off. You have earned it, richly. That's the best news out of Santa Barbara in months!'

Edward shook his head. 'At any other time, I'd be proud. Now? Hell, it's a payoff for not being killed, and not bellyaching about it. I'd have pushed it back in Bernard's face if the other Fellows hadn't been so clearly pleased; couldn't disappoint them.'

Julia said to keep the honors, as she'd force them upon him in any case. 'Therefore, go write your books, and I'll deal with Bernard Esbenshade in my own way.'

'Almost agreed, but I'm going to prove he did it, one way or another. If he killed Dr T, the police will march him off; if not,' Eddie shrugged, 'I say go easy. He's the man I thought he was: decent, dumb where Pinky is concerned, God!, but he's held the Foundation together, and deserves fair treatment until you decide on a successor. Even then, my influence, whatever it is, is in his favor.'

Frances groaned, but Julia said the sentiments did him honor, and gave Frances a look which suggested that she would do as just what she wished, whatever Edward thought. The essence of her thought was, "Men!"

Edward missed the glances, and pursued his own ideas, 'I do have a favor. Would you put Jack on the Board of Trustees? Now? He's motivated, because I told him about the possibility that Bernard killed his father.'

'You are a miracle worker! Of course Jack should be a Trustee. He was a history major, after all!'

'…and not stupid, whatever he says.'

They loaded several boxes with correspondence of Dr Ts that were in the apartment, sealed the boxes, and Edward called a shipping service and sent them on the way to Ireland.

Julia kissed him as he left, and hugged Frances, of whom she had approved.

4

IRELAND

Edward came home to what he thought of as the green cold of Ireland. To a house he liked, had been happy in, but which now, for the first time, was lonely. Bantry Bay shone with blue light in the opening at the bottom of the valley, and he wanted Frances to see it.

The double drawing room, so Greco-Roman in paired columns, twin fireplaces and swaged door frames stretched cold and untidy across the front of the house. Both rooms, furnished for academic uses with long tables, floor lamps and racks of books were lit to an icy brightness from the four long windows.

How could he work here? How had he done so before?

The vast dining room was only a little more welcoming. Eddie switched on the TV, only to hear Gaelic being read by a man with a high nervous voice. Something about God's intention to make His people grow through adversity. Eddie grimaced at that.

In the warmed kitchen, a basket of provisions filled the table. Both Mrs Barry and the Tolynals had been busy making a homecoming for him. But it wasn't enough to fill the hole of Frances' absence.

The historian worked all week on his neglected book. Index cards flew in this or that direction, references were Faxed to Dublin and Limerick for crosschecking, and the words flew through the computer and onto pages of the draft. At week's end, enough material had gone to Santa Barbara to satisfy an army of scrutinizers.

On Saturday, Frances and Eddie talked. Mutual assurances of affection were given, and, finally, a promise to appear in Dublin on the Saturday morning before Thanksgiving, three weeks off, was made by Frances. No word of apology for the harsh words of their parting in New York. Neither even remembered the fight, or perhaps anticipation erased memory.

Edward worked all the next week on the Tscherbateff outline, and fired it off on the morning he left for Dublin He was satisfied that he had put the burr under Bernard's saddle by the chapters marked, Provision for Termination of Foundation, and Tragic Death. Under the heading for Termination, he had set out all the reason's given in the original Trust Documents, provided by Julia. And, by the arrangement of other provisions for operation of the Foundation, implied all might not be well if the heirs, Jack and Julia, found fault with the operations.

Under the chapter heading, Tragic Death, he listed the topics as, "Work in progress at time Promotion of Dr Esbenshade, Investigation into causes of Explosion, and Questions remaining."

If those didn't alert Bernard that serious rumblings were afoot, nothing would. If he were innocent, he'd cry out in insulted rage. If guilty, he might show his hand by further attempting to buy Edward's silence. Or of course he might cry out in mock insult. And how will I tell the difference between one complaint and the other? Edward shrugged, and told himself he'd tried.

And then spent the rest of the week further detailing Dr T's precepts; he'd illustrate what the old boy had preached from examples from his books and letters.

On Thursday, Edward, opened the correspondence files which had come from Santa Barbara. The Foundation had sent Dr Ts dailies. Chronological folders of Dr T's outgoing correspondence, and copies of each day's incoming letters. Publications and proposed publications would have to be reviewed in Santa Barbara. Files sorted by subject matter also awaited in Santa Barbara as they often contained on-going matters, initiated in Dr T's time, and still pursued.

By putting any December's outgoing file on the worktable next to the same month's incoming file, a pretty good idea of what was going on could be formed. To follow any one correspondent was more difficult, and the first letter might not be answered for some weeks, often into the next month.

Eddie labored several days to find a system for following the thread of a series of letters. On a cardboard stand, he lettered the correspondence he wanted to track, assigning them a color. Then, as he came to, say, a Schlesinger letter, he'd flag it green, or red for a Catton letter, and so on through about twenty colors. Thus, without unclipping any one letter, he could form a pretty good idea of what needed copying and what did not.

After a further bout with Deadly History, Eddie returned to Dr T's letters. In December five years ago, a colleague from Ithaca State University had declined a Fellowship. Among his reasons was that he didn't like Bernard: "thoughtless, arrogant and in-collegial."

Amused, Eddie sought Dr T's response. Dr T had, in all other cases of criticism, responded to letters within a day or two, and usually at length. But no answer to this missive could be found within a week. Edward pulled out a perpetual calendar. The letter had come on a Wednesday. He went back to Thursday and Friday's letters directed out. Between two of Friday's letters, some wisps of copy paper adhered to a burr on the Arco Fastening. Something had worked its way out! No, may have been torn out, Eddie corrected himself.

Backing and forthing some more, Eddie found gaps in the correspondence. Letters of inquiry sent by Dr T seemed not to have been answered by the distinguished scholars to whom they had been sent. And letters critical of some publication of the Foundation's seemed not to have been answered. Only once did Eddie see any scraps of paper to support the idea that some further papers had been removed.

So, he told himself, I'm going to shock the Director's secretary, and I'm going to hope I don't give her a heart attack! Then he saw how to avoid it.

He Faxed Jamison Barker. 'Kindly hoist yourself over to campus and explain to Mrs Wells that the FAX I'm sending her tomorrow is not aimed at her, and she should make a show of demanding of Bernard what it means. Then would she please let you know? This is probably a goose chase, but may produce some results, say 50/50. And thanks!'

The FAX to Mrs Wells said, 'Are you stripping files now? Collecting data for your own biography of Dr Tscherbateff? Many gaps in the correspondence. I am sorely disappointed. I won't complain to Dr Esbenshade if you will confirm that the missing pages will be sent at once. Edward Hamilton, Senior Fellow.

Within an hour, there were three answers.

The last was the most interesting, but history must be told sequentially. Barker's FAX said, 'Mission accomplished. La Wells hugely amused, will outdo Bernhard to do in Bernard! J.B.'

La Wells Faxed, 'Dr E flounced out of here furious. I'll bet he calls you from his room. Private phone. Wouldn't do for staff to overhear Very Important Person loose his Temper! Dr E did read all of Dr Ts file when he became Director, and I believe he edited or excised that which was not flattering to himself, though I have never verified it for myself. Dr E is very sensitive to criticism, and Dr T could be rather sharp. Whatever you are doing, keep it up, and save us all. We hear Mrs Vickery is on the warpath, and gather you have same info. For God's sake don't let her close us! Not from fear of our jobs, but because we have good work to do! Que via con dios! Elizabeth C. Wells.

Bernard's call came as Eddie tore off Mrs Wells' FAX and popped it into the fire. 'What exactly are you up to Edward' Bernard Esbenshade's voice was clear and plummy.

Edward declined to admit anything.

'Now see here, our faculty is already upset by rumors spread by young Tscherbateff. I can't have you adding fuel to the conflagration! You, of all, who have the most to loose!'

'How so?'

'Your contract is safe, don't worry. It's your future I plead with you to keep unsullied. Now Edward, there is likely to be some confusion out here. Do not become involved. No one's promises can balance what I can do for you. Do you understand? Stand aloof from the controversy, and I can promise you a great future!'

'No chance, Bernard. I'm not happy, in fact I'm low as Hell about it. But I think I saw you come from turning on from creating the gas leak that blew Dr T away. And the accident I almost had is too similar for my peace of mind. Either you defend yourself to my satisfaction, or I'm not on your side. If you did nothing, I will oppose any changes in the Foundation except those that come from agreement among the Fellows and you.'

'Edward, you don't know what you are talking about. I can assure you, however, that I am not a party to what happened. Now you must believe that, and do as I say. I am perfectly willing to listen to you and the Fellows when we put Mrs Vickery's and Jack's threats behind us.'

There was a further exchange, mainly because Bernard believed that saying the same thing three times was the way to get the point over.

The whole exercise seemed puerile to Eddie as he reviewed the day. Nothing. And he still didn't believe Bernard. Or believed some of it, but felt there was an important "more" which had been unsaid.

All he had learned was that Bernard edited files as well as books. Misguided? Certainly. Evil? Criminal? Not provably. Not probably, but possibly.

In any case, I do not want to be an avenger! I'm an historian, just and only that. Yet he may lead us to the truth.

Work on the biography went quickly. Eddie found that he had an almost total recall of Dr T's concepts and methods. All, of course to be tediously researched and documented. Confidence, not new, but energizing, drove Edward day by day. He could work twelve or fourteen hours with no fatigue, and on the next day drop, without guilt, the work in hand and make for the stables. Frances up-coming visit hung above his head like a circle of light.

5

BEVERLY HILLS, California

'Hi guys, I'm Jack.' This news was received with surprise by everyone except Julia Vickery. The other Trustees simply looked at Julia for explanation, then at Bernard, who offered none, though he had a good idea of what might be coming.

The November meeting of the Trustees was in Beverly Hills. December would be in Santa Barbara, the January meeting would be in the South again. The November meeting was markedly different than any had been for many years.

A rich and elderly attorney had resigned, as Julia had asked, though she didn't say so, creating the desired vacancy. Out of order, but as explained by Julia, properly so, was Jack's election to replace the man Eddie had called Fingle-whoosis.

The financial reports were presented by the dull and correct manager from a prestigious trust company. Three hundred and forty-four million in marketable stocks and bonds, a printing factory in Indiana, the estate in California, Dr Ts copyrights books, cash and advances to historians, some of which would be recovered from publishers, and some, predictably not.

Julia asked some questions about the marketability of some long-term bonds, saying, 'Of course, I'm asking only for information. I'm not proposing that we sell them! After all, it isn't as though the Foundation were going to be wound up.' She looked at Bernard, adding ingenuously, 'Certainly not!'

Bernard merely smiled his rat's smile, and appeared unruffled.

When it was time for the Report of the Executive Director, Bernard expanded his lungs for oration, and saw Jack pick up his pencil, and hold it poised, as if to note every word Bernard might say. Concerned, but still in charge, Bernard commenced, Jack wrote furiously, and they finished together.

Without allowing a pause or addressing the Chair, Jack asked, 'Would you mind summarizing the number of publications for which the Foundation has taken responsibility, as opposed to those where the Foundation sponsored the Fellows whose work was then published by outside firms?'

Bernard hated that question. Under his management, the number of outside publications of Fellow's work had dropped precipitously. Only one risk-taker out of seven books offered during this year to date. A reversal of the days of Dr Tscherbateff, when a Fellow could get published almost on the strength that he was blessed by the Foundation. 'So much is in process, and my mind, is frankly, on working projects rather than completed ones, that I must ask Jack to come in to the office, and we'll research the question together. I welcome his interest'

Not satisfied, Jack asked, 'Isn't it true that we're more nearly a publisher of texts which no one much wants than we are the sponsors of serious scholars?'

As if on signal, Julia explained that the meeting had no provision for such sweeping question periods, and adroitly moved on to other business. The jabs had been launched, just as Edward had suggested.

Details that Bernard didn't think Trustees ought to ask had been posed. The mention had been made of a termination of the investment portfolio, waved off, but intentional, Bernard knew. And on top of the curious outline Edward had sent last Friday. Bernard knew where it was leading, where he had always known it would lead. He needed rest, and then ideas would come; ideas had always come when defense was needed. It was the absence of creative ideas that discouraged Bernard. He simply couldn't think on his feet; of ideas, he never had any. But defense? Ah, he was good at that!

Trustee Cindy Bull, until recently Mrs Cyrus Bull, neither read histories, nor wrote them, but had to fill her time. The Foundation's Trustees never met except on Friday's, and that for Julia Armbruster Vickery's convenience in flying from New York, so it balanced Cindy's week. She glanced at her nails, thought an evil thought about her manicurist, and turned to the problem that her mentor on this board had resigned. He'd said that Julia had asked him to go, to make room for Jack Tscherbateff. What's a boy who's dressed for clam digging doing here? Absolutely no dignity. But very good looks, if you like juveniles, she sniffed. Herself next? That would be embarrassing.

Under New Business, Cindy Auchterarder Bull said, 'Madam Chair, I find my duties at the Philharmonic, and other charities take so much of my time, that I wonder if you would permit me to tender my resignation?'

Amid crocodile tears, the board accepted the resignation of the ex-wife of the richest man anyone knew, as well as any hope of additional endowment from the Auchterarder estate, or from Bull himself.

Jack recognized himself, saying, 'Is this the place? I mean the time to designate a Trustee to replace Mrs Bull.'

It was not, but Julia and Jack had discussed the possibility of finding another opening on the board, and knew exactly what Jack would say. When he had said it, Bernard claimed the floor.

Madam Chairman, 'I am very proud to nominate our new Senior Fellow to this board, Dr Edward Hamilton.' Bernard was not, however he felt, about to show that he could be upstaged. Quite outside the order of her agenda, Julia accepted the nomination, put it to the predictable vote of ayes, and closed the meeting with considerable satisfaction.

In the motor court of the Beverly Wilshire Hotel where the meeting had been held, Jack buttonholed Bernard, to load another problem on him, 'I didn't see any item about repairing the cottage where Eddie Hamilton was gassed. I thought that was the reason you got old Dr Randall out. Or was there another reason?'

Impassivity. 'Small accident. I'll never forgive that I had asked Dr Randall to vacate so we could get on with the repairs, and then allowed Dr Hamilton to use it during his too-brief stay.'

Bernard stopped Jack in his tracks by then saying, 'You will be surprised to know that we share exactly the same feelings about Edward!'

Jack felt he'd been rude with no purpose when it seemed that his jibe about the explosion had glanced off Bernard unnoticed. Jack would have felt better if he'd seen the mistake Bernard made at the end of the driveway. Would have known that he'd hit a nerve.

Bernard drove north in the same trance as had allowed his wrong-way turn into the one-way street outside the Beverly Wilshire's motor court. Cars passed him on the Coast Highway, while he crept along at fifty-five and less, through the coast towns, into Montecito, Santa Barbara's version of the Forest Lawn of the living. The Foundation's neighborhood is so exclusive that street addresses are purposely hidden within deep hedges, and curbs or sidewalks never intrude, nor, indeed, street lighting.

Bernard had only one idea. Edward must be brought around, made to help him.

Edward's carefully composed chapter in the Tscherbateff book, had come in on e-mail early Friday morning. Been in the In-Box when Bernard entered his office at eight-thirty. He had read it quickly before he left for Beverly Hills. And he had had it in mind when he sat at the Board meeting.

Bernard had no idea that Edward had labored intensely to expand Leila Armbruster Tscherbateff's intentions for the Foundation; an expansion which was undocumented and perhaps fanciful...highly unprofessional. Or that Edward had also cribbed Dr T's comments on quite another occasion. Where Dr T had sternly lectured Congress on their duty to leave think-tank foundations unfettered, Edward had extrapolated and convoluted what Tscherbateff had said. Made it seem a threat aimed at Dr T's successors.

As the transcripts of Congressional testimony had come from Julia, and dated back to before the Foundation had been created, Bernard could not really know, from Santa Barbara, whether Dr T had said it or not. The cribbing of phrases was so skillful that it sounded very like the rolling phrases that Bernard so haplessly imitated.

Bernard decided to go to Ireland. To neutralize Edward, to smooth the conflict that he saw brewing, and which would unseat him, and perhaps threaten the Foundation. He would go on Thanksgiving weekend, when it was normal for the Director to visit in Palm Springs.

6

IRELAND Thanksgiving Week

At last, Francis came to Dublin on the Friday that began Thanksgiving week. They spent the night at the Shelbourne, intending to tour Dublin, before heading south to Bantry. The same Friday when, in Beverly Hills, Edward had been elected to the Board of Trustees.

Very early on Saturday morning, which meant late Saturday in Beverly Hills, Julia Vikery's telephone call interrupted their post-coital glow.

She also passed on the news of Edward's election to the Board, about which she was pleased. She also reported Jack's questions, but said she had no idea how deeply or accurately they hit Bernard. 'Easter Island face, the whole time. But he actually took the words away from Jack, and made a pretty speech about you as he nominated you. Seemed just as though it was his whole idea.'

Eddie turned from the phone to Frances, and reported that he was displeased. 'I'm drawn into their fight! I never wanted to be on the Board, and I sure as Hell want off it as soon as we straighten up the two issues!'

By which Frances understood him to mean the cause of Dr T's death, the reasons for his promotion. For him the future of the Foundation was still in the Board's hands, not his. Again, Frances felt an unreasonable surge of…what? Adrenaline? She understood how to fight this battle. Why couldn't Eddie! He was capable. Had guts. Just watch him push a horse over a wall! He had determination, because she'd watched him reduce ten index cards to a single paragraph, and include all that was in the cards. Why keep hiding from what was clearly his duty? And an opportunity as well.

This time Francis said nothing. Willed herself to relax. Maybe Eddie wasn't a fighter, he was a fair man, temperate and wise in lots of ways. And she could be the fighter for both of them! Put her on that Board, and she'd have Bernard begging to be allowed to quit!

Frances read the pretended chapter, the outline that had alarmed Bernard, late Sunday. They'd tramped all day, and had intended a pub meal and early bedtime. But no, anywhere they thought that they would like was closed. Sunday! The Shelbourne Hotel cared for its guests, but cared enough that rough sightseeing clothes would not do for dinner. While she read, Eddie to bellowed his way through a shower and shave.

Regular walrus, she reflected.

Pretty subtle writing, this bogus chapter, but might go over with an academic type like Bernard. Clever, in fact. As they dined in the quiet Edwardian glow of the Dining Room, she asked, 'Are you sure? Did they really say all that? I mean about breaking the whole thing up?

'No, but that's what's likely to get Bernard on the defensive. The only real part is what I've said about Leila's power to wind it up.'

'But he already knows that. It's in the documentation...the Charter.'

Eddie explained that he needed to force Bernard's hand. Get a wedge into him which might wring out a confession, or at the least, be sure there were changes in the editing and publication policies of the Foundation. 'It must be the publisher of last resort, not simply a printing press to turn out a string of pedantical index cards!'

Actually, they spent two days in Dublin, then on Monday, by way of Powerscourt and Castletown House, they drove easily down to Waterford and on towards Bantry Bay.

Frances praised the double drawing room, 'I'd never have thought that such formal rooms could be so attractive! It must be the writer's mess which you've used for decoration!' And the great square dining room, with an ancient wing chair as a host chair at the table, she liked equally well.

There was e-mail from Bernard: Urgent we speak, and much regret I could not reach you on Saturday. Please be available to speak on Wednesday evening. Your friend, JBE.

'He writes a FAX like we used to write telegrams! Oh Bernard! He's hard to hate...'

Frances asked if he always signed himself "Your friend" 'Sounds so Sherlock Holmes.'

Eddie thought the whole FAX strange. Why not just have announced his election to the Board of Trustees, and take the credit for it himself if he wanted to. Or, if he wanted to actually talk, why not tell Eddie to call Monday, or 'at once' or however he wanted to say it. But Wednesday? Evening? Three days after he sent it?

Tuesday was given over to the horses at the farm of one of Edward's neighbors, the Tolynals. Frances rode with effortless grace, endearing herself thereby to Eddie all the more. His tall frame dominated whatever horse he rode, while hers complemented the beast. Gently at first, and then cantering, they took small walls and fences in easy tandem, and, at last, galloped flat out down a long lane, to end laughing and out of breath at a pub far from Bantry Bay.

In the dark bar, they had pub lunch and unbearably sweet ginger ale, rounded out with pickles and relish. And laughed at nothing, and held hands, and longed to be home and undressed and together.

In the evenings, of course, they were together, raided the refrigerator, and were together again, and perhaps, who knows, again.

One night they dined with the Tolynals in some state at Tollynoll House. Georgian practically everything, Frances saw.

When she asked why the house name was spelled differently than the family name, she heard a long Irish tale about loosing the house in the 19th century, emigrating to England, falling into 'trade', and changing the family spelling for English convenience. When, after 1922, rcal estate prices fell, the family bought back their own house, and preserved the story of their return in the spelling of the two names.

After the story was told, they all made excited plans for the Thanksgiving, the first the Tolynals had ever celebrated.

Walking home over the knoll in the still chill, Frances held Eddie's gloved hand and thought private thoughts. She was convinced that this was the man for her. But not that she ought to let such conviction end her legal career. An impending partnership in the law firm was too important to miss. Too much thinking, she considered, was probably a bad thing. Still, the matter of self-interest required that Eddie affiliate with Columbia or NYU, or, less conveniently Yale or

Princeton, so that her career could go on uninterrupted. After all, it can't matter where a historian writes his books, can't?

Then she thought of Eddie walking close beside her, laughing his rare loud laugh as she stumbled almost into his arms. And of Eddie at his desk that sun-lit morning, bent over some letters, making notes, a beatific expression as he understood something Dr T had implied. He'd said, 'Here, Dr T actually says he doesn't like Bernard. `Our Bernard is at his usual business of putting down; it won't do.' Vintage Dr T.'

Her thoughts went back to morning. Eddie had said, 'I think the missing letters would confirm that Dr T was on to Bernard's holier than thou stuff; I always wondered.'

Frances had asked if Dr T had intended Bernard to succeed him.

'I don't know. He's a good caretaker, and I guess valued for that. Still, I've seen flashes in Dr T's letters to the trustees, and especially to Julia, of dislike. Resentment, more like, but this is the first I've seen in a letter to a colleague. To Barett of University of Chicago.'

Remembering Eddie's face as he worked, Frances forgot all about a New York career, and moved her mind to a big untidy house where she would watch Eddie at work, and were those small feet pattering about?

Then the lawyer's mind cut in: we'll find a compromise. I'll practice in a country town, and he can work in my office. No, I can work from the house.

Wednesday evening the telephone did not ring. Eddie called Santa Barbara, but no, Bernard was away for the weekend, had left Tuesday, probably for Palm Springs. 'Do you want the number there?' But there was no point. Bernard had said he'd call. Let him do it.

They rose late on Thanksgiving morning. He had to say welcome to Frances, didn't he? In a way which lovers would understand.

A brief canter while the turkey cooked. Fresh cool air, scented woods, wafts of wood smoke from cottages and country houses busy on, what is to them, an ordinary workday. Eddie spoke briefly with Tolynal, who said he had not seen any more lurkers, and, long finger at the side of his nose, asked 'Any luck?'

'What?'

'You know, coaxing Francis to move here. I know she's holding out about it. Why not try the old proposal of marriage; Mary Seana says it is the best persuader.'

'Tell you later…' Edward slid away, not ready to be rushed into anything. Things between Frances and Eddie were just fine; why monkey with perfection?

The Tolynals and kits and pots and pans arrived fragrantly at six o'clock. The men found whiskey, the two women white wine, and the kidlets, a TV that accepted their video. Alone with Eddie in the long untidy, Tolynal reverted to the line of comment he'd initiated at the stable.

'Hold it.' Edward said, 'We're not near an engagement, let alone a wedding!'

'Says you. Look here, Mary Seana and I have a proprietary interest in you two. Can't afford to loose the board of two horses. Rather have you settle down here, under our eye, don't you see.'

Eddie shook his head.

'Believe me, marriage is the right thing for a buck like you. That solitary life was turning you into a grouch. Not like now, you're much more,' Tolynal waved his hand negligently, 'more civilized, I guess.'

While Edward mopped up his laugh at that, Frances declared dinner to be served.

Mounds of something called 'Swedes and mash' sent clouds of buttery-creamy smells from the buffet. The turkey, appearing in its most American style, chestnut dressing and cranberry sauce, fascinated the children. Faced with it, Edward declared that he hadn't met an un-carved bird before. Tolynal's goose-slicing technique was employed, and Frances said it met American standards.

The adults lingered at table, passing port, nuts and smelly cheese until nearly ten. When the telephone rang.

Edward went into the drawing room, spoke for some time and returned, spreading his hands wide, lifting his shoulders. 'Why,' he said, 'would Bernard wait until ten to call me?

Practically two in the afternoon on the West Coast. On a holiday?'

'Well, saying what?' Frances leaned forward, eager to hear.

'Offered me the Executive Directorship of the Foundation!'

To the Tolynals he said, 'Headship. Boss-stuff!'

'Good on! Well done. Let's have a toast to that!' the visitors chorused.

Frances continued to look at Edward, almost sure of what was to come.

'Sorry guys. I nixed it; declined the honor.'

Groans.

'He gave me a big ruffle-and-flourish about what I've written. Said I've outlined Tscherbateff's career brilliantly, and can now hand it over to a bio-writer, a ghost, to finish. "Soon as you complete the Deadly History, I will step aside and allow you to assume the mantle of responsibility for the foundation." Fat chance.'

Edward mimicked the sonorities of Bernard's diction. "I will, of course, continue as Director-Emeritus, but that will represent no inconvenience for you, upon which you may place utter reliance."' Eddie shrugged, 'In other words, lay off the biography, and you may have ice-cream for desert!'

'Pardon?' said Tolynal, 'New idiom?'

'Scrambled imagery.' said Edward.

Frances walked around behind Eddie, ran her hands soothingly over his shoulders. 'What Eddie has not told you is that the Chairperson of the Foundation called Eddie Sunday morning. The Trustees elected him to their board!'

'Scrambled.' Eddie said. They elected me to a Trusteeship composed of over-seers and financial blots. Honorary. And I mean it to be temporary. Bernard is just trying to buy me off. Again.'

Frances bopped Eddie gently on both shoulders with her fists. 'Did it ever occur to you that you deserve all this? That Bernard may, for once be sincere?'

Eddie suggested kindly that Frances needed her head examined, and drew her around and into his lap, handing her some champagne as he did so.

Talynal said, 'I hope that your attitude isn't related to a deception of mine. You see, the spy I reported to you was just that, but regretfully he was our spy! A spook of my own government. They read your article, and rather thought it sounded too good to be quite true. So some counter-jumper nipped down to have a closer look. Sorry, but I was disinclined to admit what ignoramuses we employ!' He moved his dark head around to include his wife, 'And we should be crushed if my silence has led you to 'nix' as you say, the offer.'

Frances asked, 'Is that all Bernard said?'

Glad to have the spy thing out of the way, Eddie ignored Frances and asked why the Irish government was so protective of Tolynal. But Tolynal couldn't or wouldn't answer, just shook his head, index finger to his mouth. Eddie shrugged: spy stuff he thought.

Frances wouldn't be diverted, 'Is that all Bernard said?'

'Not quite. After I declined to take his bait, he said, "This decision has most serious consequences to all of us. I am unable to continue as Executive Director; only you can defend your colleagues, and I do not conceive that your conscience would fail in that challenge." And he hung up.'

'Damn if I see it, Edward. Are you saying that unless he also gives up the Director-Emeritus post, you won't take the headship?' Tolynal shook his head again. Executive Directorships meant pay-slips, and the Tolynals of Tollynoll House could do with a few of those.

'Look old buddy, you have two big opinions about me tonight. Ever so gently,' and Edward's face softened as he leaned confidentially toward Tolynal, 'would you stuff it?'

In general hilarity, the party broke up, and the house settled to November quiet.

Around eleven on Friday morning, as Frances and Edward stood in the vestibule fastening riding jackets, hunt caps, gloves and scarves, a car approached along the drive. The sunlight, low in the sky, silhouetted the passenger. Not until the car had stopped opposite them in the drive, and the driver pulled himself out, did they realize it was Bernard!

He was sorry to intrude. Had called last night from Dublin, as soon as he arrived. Was upset by Edward's attitude. Settled in the drawing room, he waited for Frances to leave. 'Not going.' she said, 'Staying. You need me.'

Bernard shrugged. 'My mission is very grave. I am prepared to cut short my life's work that you may have time to save the Foundation from a rapacious raid by Jack Tscherbateff and his step-sister. They have teamed to offset my majority on the Board of Trustees. They have floated veiled hints about declining academic standards, and worse, about misfeasance in using research data.'

'You want me to believe that they want to revoke the Foundation's grant? And if they did, why? Julia has more than enough money to live on forever, and Jack has no ambition beyond the next set of waves. No, I think they have a real concern about the way you run things, and what you have done to keep control. Let alone done to gain control in the first place!'

Bernard narrowed his eyes, steepled his fingers across his not-very prominent belly.

'Yes, Edward, you are clever. But not really clever enough. All these ideas of my sins were put in your mind by the two people who benefit by bringing me to the dust.'

'Sorry. They didn't see you the night Dr T was killed. I did. You were walking up the south path. I thought at the time you were walking from the swimming pool, where Pinky had been. I thought you were coming back from looking for Pinky.

'But no, I think you were coming back from blowing up Dr T!'

Bernard did the most unexpected thing. He began to cry. Tears formed on his lower lids, followed gravity down the lines by his mouth, seemed to shine his chin. Not sobbing, grief-induced tears. Rather the overflowing of long sadness.

As he did not move, nor grimace, nor even seem aware of what had occurred, Frances brought water, a napkin, and held the glass to Bernard's mouth, put the cloth in his hands.

Edward sat still as well, not understanding the reaction: I tell him I know he's a murderer, and he weeps?

'I must tell it all, I see. Heaven forbid that I have come to this pass.' Bernard's voice was smaller, as he himself seemed. 'You have known, Edward, that I am not a scholar of the standing of our colleagues. Indeed not even of the standing of some scholars whom I have heard you disparage. I have, however, tried to impart a certain style to our work, a unity of expression, that the Foundation's work would stand as a recognized body. You have opposed that, I know. Jack expressed your very own views at the Trustees meeting.'

Edward acknowledged all that, not saying that the starched and opaque prose style of the Foundation's publications was their greatest fault. Not scholarship, and not the range of subject matter. 'So go on with it, if you're going to confess.'

'I have perhaps seemed vain, perhaps swaggering, in the discharge of my duties. But we could gain no prestige with Dr Ts tweedy disorder; he had no standards except academic ones.'

Eddie couldn't let him finish. 'He had enough for a great man. Whom you did intentionally, and with the most foul of motives, kill.'

Bernard shuddered, moved his body from side to side, saying softly, 'Quite obviously, you believe that I contrived to blow up Dr John Tscherbateff's cottage, thus killing him. And that my motive was the succession to his position. That I did not do, I assure you.'

Edward writhed in his chair in disgust, flung Frances a harsh look.

Frances spoke for the first time, 'We'd like to believe you, but you know, you must tell us what did happen before we can do that.'

'Edward knows that I sought my daughter, then his wife. Maud, whom he called Pinky. I thought it would be easier on both Edward and Maud if I found her rather than if Edward did.'

Thanks for nothing.

'She was in the pool pavilion, quite undressed, insensible and chilled so that she was as cold as marble. I gathered her up, and staggered to Dr Tscherbateff's door, the closest cottage. I banged until he let me in. He lit the gas fire, we wrapped her in blankets, and he kindly said he would make some hot tea. He stepped into the dressing room to do so, then came back for matches. At that point, Maud came to consciousness, and, seeing Dr Tscherbateff, vituperated him with every objurgatory phrase she had picked up on the beaches and in the lowest bars of Santa Barbara.'

Bernard fumbled for the water, which Frances passed to him. 'Her words were so unjustified that Dr T stepped back, shocked as you know so gentle a man would be. He said "I'm so sorry for this, Bernard" and stepped into his bedroom.'

'Sorry for this?' Frances prompted.

'For me, he meant, for Maud. He was the most scrupulously polite man.'

'And you left Pinky there?'

'No…not at all. She rose, unsteadily you may as well know, and clasped the blanket about herself. A white blanket. And left the cottage. And so did I.'

'Leaving the gas logs turned on?'

'I reproach myself, I did. And I fear that flame ignited the fumes from the little hot plate in the dressing room, which Dr T had turned on before he came in to us for a match.'

'By God! You didn't kill Dr T! Jesus have I made an ass of all of us. God, what a mess I've made.' Eddie was even more upset than he said he was. Then, his mind pictured Bernard alone on the path. He reddened and said, 'But you were alone on the path when I saw you?'

Maud had gone on ahead, Bernard explained in about a hundred badly chosen words.

'What's the truth of it? Dr T told you to send Pinky away. Right? Did you intend to do it?'

'The truth? He said either she went or we both went.'

Bernard sighed deeply. 'But there was no place she could go. She knew she had to stay with me! It was working. I was able to shame her out of her behavior. She was getting better!'

'You shamed her? The way you shame the Fellows into your ideas of syntax and literary style?'

'Well, I expect so. I have some success at the application of wit to pedagogy, probably.'

Sarcasm, rebuke, inducement of feelings of guilt and self-disgust, Eddie could imagine it! Poor Pinky!

'Yet she continued to be rebellious, as you yourself observed. She had been keeping company with Senator Lindblad, but she outraged even him.'

'He died in a car accident, in Montecito, coming back from a party, didn't he?'

'Not precisely. No, your Pinky became involved in a fight with him on the way home. She shot at him, missed. Her pearl-handled pistol was a silly thing, but had she intended damage, she could easily have inflicted it. In avoiding the tussle, he careened off of Mountain Drive, smashing his car. Pinky climbed out, walked down to the Foundation, and slept off her condition. Unfortunately, she slept while Senator Lindblad bled to death. So she was complicit in two deaths, you see.'

'And you used humor and barbs to shame her again?'

'Well, I suppose so. I felt she had to make amends to society, you see. Not that the authorities really knew what had happened; they actually supposed that the Senator had left her at the Foundation and then tried to return to the party.'

'And you backed her story?' Frances was incredulous.

'Naturally. It would not have been good for the Foundation otherwise. And I took her pistol from her; I have it in my bags, as a matter of fact, so there's no more danger there!'

The winter sun had fallen away from the long south-facing windows, and the room became cool. Francis and Edward were still in outdoor clothes, but Bernard was clearly feeling the chill. Edward hopped to, built and lit fires in both fireplaces, and Frances left to stir up some tea and leftovers. Bernard looked exhausted, and for that both of them felt pity.

Bernard ate some turkey sandwiches, explaining that Thanksgiving dinner on Aer Lingus had been salmon or breaded meat, and smiled ruefully.

Then he leaned back. 'And of course, Maud resented being left by you at your convenience, and took the opportunity to be even with you by an attempt on your life in Dr Randall's cottage.'

'You mean, he wasn't moved out so you could stage an accident for me?'

'Goodness sakes, we had been trying to shift the good doctor for a year. He was simply inert. No, I merely used the housekeeper's suggestion. She respects you, you know, and thought the cottage would be more pleasant for you for your visit.' Than a room near Pinky Mrs Loesch had meant, but could not articulate.

'As for conniving to succeed Dr Tscherbateff, you are right. I had been grooming you as our principal historian, and, had Dr T lived he would have come all the way to my conclusion. You are an unique talent. You are on the edge of fame, of the prestige the Foundation needs. From my perspective, Dr T died too soon. You were hardly in the line of succession! Most carefully,

I enlisted Jamison Barker. Told him it would have to be me for an interim of three or four years, then I would yield to you.'

Again, Eddie consulted the egg-and-dart moldings of the ceiling, searching for the patience to believe so patent a lie.

Bernard wasn't to be stopped. He'd said whatever needed saying to each Trustee, and talked them out of hiring a national search firm. 'An hiatus would discourage important publications,' he had asserted. Which, he admitted, may have backfired when Julia realized that none were forthcoming.

'I needed time to get your next book in print. I've been sending most of your material on to your publisher, you didn't know that, did you?'

Frances knew Bernard had that right. The right to manage a Fellow's publications during the term of the Fellowship. Although the work belonged to the Fellow, the Foundation, as sponsor,controlled it.

'I expect you will soon receive a proposal from your publisher that will please you enormously. An advance, which is heroic, is proposed, and a minimum first printing of an hundred thousand copies! My judgement has been vindicated!'

He had Eddie's full attention. And belief. How could it be false? His publisher popped for a hundred thousand in the first run? Now that was Belief!

Both Frances and Edward were as kind to Bernard as they could be, given that both disliked the man. At bedtime, Bernard reverted to his invitation of the night before. 'I intend to take Maud away with me. Oh, she'll go. And I hope to get her into a residential rehabilitation program in South Carolina. In any case, she will not return to the Foundation, I can guarantee that. And so can you guarantee it, for you will be in charge.'

'Sorry. No dice. Nothing doing. My job is to write. I'm no administrator, and never will be. Sorry, Bernard,' and to his credit, Edward placed his large hand on Bernard's narrow shoulder, and squeezed encouragingly.

Bernard told a circular sort of story of his stewardship of the foundation. He had begun his Directorship without confidence, feeling the job was temporary. He had chosen Edward to succeed him, and had set him up to do so. The remote haven for scholarship, the visits by his colleagues increased his stature. The success of his published works was understood and enjoyed by all the Fellows. The clamor for Edward's succession was now universal, and Bernard welcomed it. 'I have done my best to assure the consensus.'

For Edward to deny his future was wrong, Bernard insisted.

'Destiny knocks, and you must answer,' he concluded in the tones of Polonius dragging out another platitude.

Eddie sat very quietly, listening. But his expression was unknowable. Not set against Bernard, but not showing anything. Frances saw the pulse along his jaw, but it revealed nothing to her. Except that she saw how wrong she had been about Eddie. He had incredible strength. He was a moral man.

His success must come in a way that Edward regarded as right or he would not have it!

The moral man will not avail himself of any opportunity come by in an unsavory manner. Bernard had arranged matters by conniving to protect the pneumatic Pinky, all the while planning Eddie's advancement. Both causing Eddie to reject his future.

Bernard looked even more dejected. Into the long silence, Bernard said, 'Oh Edward, that is the end of the Foundation. I will be unable to withstand the pressure.'

'Sorry, I'm almost convinced that closing down is the right thing. We can talk it over tomorrow…'

'Good God, I talked as though I had something to do with it. With the Foundation's future.' Eddie had his head comfortably on the pillow, close to Frances. 'I've brought down the whole damn thing! And all I really wanted was Dr T's ideas to be respected. Recognized.'

Frances said that in any case, his grant couldn't be cancelled, and he'd finish both Deadly History and A New View of the Historian, and to rest easy, he was doing the right thing. Of the latter, Frances wasn't sure, but her man had done it, so it was her job, lawyer or lover, to be sure that it seemed right.

Then Edward said, almost in a whisper, 'Pinky killed Dr T. Poor Bernard! He knows it, and it's agony to him. She wasn't ahead of him. White blanket! I'd have seen that, I know I would have. He left her in the cottage, to sleep it off.'

'And she didn't. What a mess…' And, somehow they slept.

Early on the day Saturday after Thanksgiving, Frances and Eddie went softly downstairs and out to the kitchen. They had Irish bread, coffee and some jam sent from Tollynoll House, and left a fine spread and a thermos for Bernard, who'd been tucked into the guestroom the night before. They rode two of Tolynal's horses along the ridges, sparkling blue sea on one side, green, endless fields and spinneys on the other.

When the sun was respectably approaching mid-day, they returned to the house. Bernard's car was where it had been the night before, next to the front door.

They went in through the kitchen, to find the thermos and soda bread were as they had been left. The house silent.

Silence above, as well. Jet lag? Bernard was in his sixties, not so decrepit. Frances showered and changed, and at noon persuaded Eddie that the silence bore looking into. He knocked at Bernard's door, and called out, and finally opened the door to show a perfectly made bed, utterly neat bureau, and Bernard's luggage, carefully stacked at the foot of the bed.

Alarmed, Eddie went down to the front door, and out to the car. Where Bernard sat in the passenger seat. Motionless, an insignificant pearl handled pistol in his still hand, the scarab ring answering the daylight with a dull gleam. The red wound in his right temple seemed easily patched, but the damage on the driver's side of the car told of his death otherwise.

Neatly paper-clipped to the lowered visor, a note carefully folded, and inscribed, 'For Edward Hamilton, PhD, Senior Fellow, Trustee.'

Eddie read the note twice, sitting the second time on the damp bench by the front door. Hopeless prose; dead as poor Bernard. Eddie found the message appalling in tone and content.

Frances came out, saw the open car door, said 'What?'

'Shot himself. Neat as you please about it too. And this...,' he said, handing her the note.

Frances read into the soft winter breeze, 'I have but one hope, which is to force you to your destiny, although I know only too well that responsibility can not be given, only taken up by those who should bear those burdens. Nevertheless, I urge you, from beyond this world, to return to the Foundation and accept your duties. Help Maud if you are able so to do.'

'Good lord! How not to influence people or win friends!'

'Poor man!'

'More convincing than you think,' but Eddie would not be drawn out further.

The Garda Sergeant agreed that Bernard's death was suicide, but his team took as much time over it as though it had been murder. Thorough, sympathetic, helpful. Miraculously, the police surgeon gave a Death Certificate on the spot. Export papers would be available the following Monday. And the pearl-handled pistol would be sent on, with the rest of Bernard's possessions to his home in California. No, Dr Hamilton could not ship them, and the Garda rather indicated that he suspected Edward had some sinister design to seize and possess himself of them. They must be mailed to California, not carried.

When the Gardai and the ambulance had left, dark was falling, and the Tolynal's descended with soup, leftovers and spirits. Apparently Tolynal had been briefed at the start of the proceedings, and had facilitated matters beyond the usual Irish courtesy to travelers.

'Me? Use influence? Aye, no, haven't got an ounce of it.' Tolynal laid his index finger alongside of his nose.

The results were clear: Edward was free to leave Ireland from the moment the Garda turned down the driveway.

No one, however, could get any reaction from Eddie about Bernard's last wishes.

7

SANTA BARBARA The Special Meeting

The Special Meeting of the Trustees, on the 30th of November, went predictably.

Eddie was elected to the Directorship of the Foundation, over his avowed lack of commitment. He only promised to review current activities and decide whether to recommend either a closing of the campus, or a rededication. Nor would he promise to remain Director if the Foundation was to continue. In brief, he received a free hand.

Whatever he had said to the Trustees was a strategy, however. The moral man was determined to do whatever it took to put the Foundation back on its feet. If he had to endure scandal along the way, he would, but if it could be avoided, so much the better.

The corduroys were not unpacked. Today, Edward wore a gray suit, lighter gray shirt and a steel-colored necktie: dead serious. He'd got freedom by dissembling his determination. The moral man?

Eddie ought to have been chuffed by the exuberant congratulations of the Fellows, staff and Trustees, but was not. He had a task to do, and would not allow flattery to influence him.

Frances, however was charmed by the academic compliments. She was in fact revising her ideas about what sort of career she should have.

Pinky, who'd been hovering woozily, asked if he wanted '…any help sorting this place out? Believe me, I know how to keep this gang,' she gestured at the scholars, 'in line. Better believe it!' At the end of her gesture, Eddie saw Bernard's heavy scarab ring. The luggage from Ireland had arrived, he saw, and the ring, last seen on Bernard's hand, had an especially evil look on Pinky's soft hand.

'We'll talk, but I'd make some plans, Pinky, if I were you.' Eddie smiled to show a friendly intention. He didn't feel friendly, but then he'd decided to avoid scandal. A decision hard fought within himself. Much as he preferred to see her punished, it was a principal he had to give up. He needed special freedom to deal with this, he knew. And he heard Bernard's voice with an ear re-tuned, 'It wouldn't be good for the Foundation.' An un-provable crime…

Pinky's guilt, if it could be proven, was a divagation. Eddie wouldn't be distracted by it, and he wouldn't have the Trustees diverted by it, either.

Enough for Pinky to scram, and suffer whatever pangs of remorse she might feel off-campus. She surely seemed to have no feelings about her father's death, and she resented Edward's intentions.

Pinky wasn't out yet! 'Watch it, Mister Big. Jack's thinking he's white meat for my sandwich! I just may be moving over there. So just think what I can do…' Her chin went back, and her breasts bobbed high; he had a flash that she'd overbalance herself...

Frances saw, but didn't hear Pinky's threat.

Mrs Loesch, who knew the gesture, steered Pinky back towards the bar. Mrs Loesch had had a discussion with Edward that morning.

The open bar arrangements for the scholars was simply an inexpensive courtesy, as they rarely drank much more than the wine served with dinner. The courtesy had been a subsidy to Pinky, who abused it. Mrs Loesch made sure that Edward understood that Dr Esbenshade regularly contributed to the house account to cover the imbalance in consumption. And now, what should she do? Edward said he'd take care of the problem, and Mrs Loesch didn't pursue it. In general, she appreciated that Edward hadn't changed any of the Foundation's domestic policies.

Edward's Inaugural Luncheon went forward with great pomp. Distinguished professors from two state universities, and from The University of Southern California and Stanford attended, adding their congratulations along the way.

Pinky sat next to an uncomfortable looking Jack, and clung to his arm so as to impede his use of knife and fork.

'What are you going to do with that...' Mrs Dr. Middleton glanced at Pinky and Jack who whispered together, rancorously. Pinky reached for and downed Jack's wine.

'She's going to her aunt in Chicago, I think,' Eddie said smoothly, as if unconcerned. On his other side, Dr Randall spoke quietly, 'I believe I will follow Miss Esbenshade into retirement as well. I like you too well to contemplate being in any way a hindrance to your work here.'

Eddie took Randall's hand between his own two large hands, and assured him that his intention was otherwise. 'Yes, we're going to be so good that our books will be published because they came from our Fellows, but we will always self-publish the specialized high quality books which you write. And I need your advice anyway.'

At length, the luncheon party broke up. Eddie stood at the main door to the house, bidding Trustees and visitors good-bye, while the Resident Fellows and senior staff spread along the entry porch.

Jack Tscherbateff had folded himself into a small red sports car parked in the broad reddish sweep of the driveway. Sunlight filtered through over-arching fronds of rare palm trees, giving an impressionist sort of light to the scene.

Pinky, had followed Jack. As he backed out of his space, she raised her voice. Jack shook his head, and turned it to finish the backing out.

'...muscle-bound cretin...' she said clearly. Some laughed a little, but the pop of a revolver shot cut short all other sound. Jack fell sidewise, and the car accelerated backwards into someone's station wagon.

Into the echo, Pinky turned awkwardly, and let off four more bullets in the general direction of the house. The shots raised a little cloud of earth near the porch, clanged on a metal stanchion, thunked into the house, and, sickeningly, called a gasp from Dr Medina, who fell backwards into a sitting position on the flagstones of the porch.

Before the fifth shot was squeezed off, Eddie was across the driveway, intending to take the pistol from Pinky. She aimed directly at him, and made the last shot count. But not for enough, from her point of view.

'Nice clean shot,' the ambulance driver commented. Edward smiled at Frances who was saying, 'Edward, Edward dearest!'

And then he passed comfortably out, remembering Pinky being tackled from the sidelines by that intrepid scholar of the Byzantine labyrinths of intrigue, Dr Randall!

ABOUT THE AUTHOR

Distinguished wit and bon vivant, novelist Richard Crissman has contributed to MONEY MAGAZINE and various publications of the National Trust for Historic Preservation and the Potomac Institute. His offbeat novels are about money and what it does to people: the power, the self-indulgence and the glamour! He shares the secrets of making, keeping and managing vast fortunes.

His characters are eccentric, foolish, and very human: nuts and nuggets. His plots are unexpected and as American as P. G. Wodehouse's plots were top-drawer British. His heroes are single-minded horsemen like those of Dick Francis, and they never forget what they want.

Crissman and his elegant wife live in Southern California, very much part of the milieu of which he writes.

9 781583 487785